Mane glinting like forward.

Jinx looked away, swishing his black tail in apparent boredom, though Sam would bet he was still watching the stallion from the corner of his eye. Why didn't he retreat?

When Jinx held his ground, the Phantom lowered his head into a herding position. His shoulder muscles bunched as he advanced. The gelding sidestepped, eyes rolling.

Suddenly aware that Jake was rummaging around in the truck, Sam pried her gaze from the horses.

"What are you doing?" she asked.

"Getting out. Your horse is gonna drive that gelding back this way. When he does, I'll rope him."

"I'm coming with you," Sam said, but the truck door had just closed when the Phantom charged.

Read all the books about the

Phantom Stallion

Phantom Stallion

∾ 13 ∾
Heartbreak Bronco

TERRI FARLEY

AVON BOOKS

An Imprint of HarperCollins*Publishers*

Library of Congress Catalog Card Number:
2003098432
ISBN 0-06-058314-2

First Avon edition, 2004

AVON TRADEMARK REG. U.S. PAT. OFF. AND IN OTHER COUNTRIES,
MARCA REGISTRADA, HECHO EN U.S.A.

Visit us on the World Wide Web!
www.harperchildrens.com

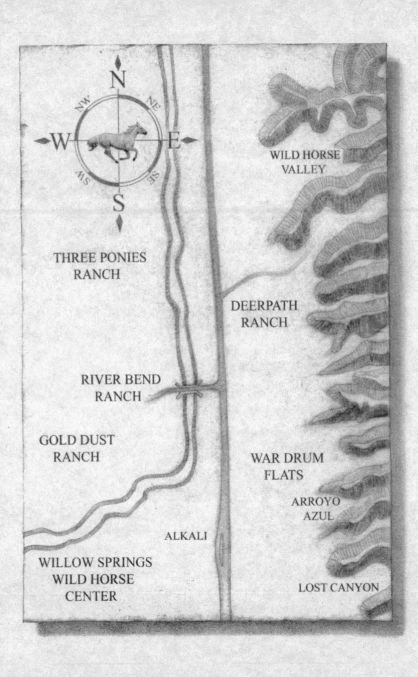

Chapter One ∾

𝒯he faded wall banner that proclaimed Clara's coffee shop "Home of the Best Pineapple Upside-Down Cake in the World!" fluttered as the ceiling fan turned lazily overhead.

The fan stirred wisps of Samantha Forster's reddish hair as she tilted her head back and closed her eyes. It was barely noon on an early June day, but before driving into Darton with her dad, she'd put in a full morning of work with the horses on River Bend Ranch.

"Don't nod off, now," warned a rusty female voice Sam recognized as Clara's. "Lunch is here."

Sam smelled the giant cheeseburgers and french fries before she opened her eyes to see them.

"Not a chance," she said.

Sitting across the table from her, Dad rubbed his palms together. His sun-browned face creased in a smile as Clara positioned plates in front of each of them.

"Guess Sam's enjoyin' her last afternoon of peace and quiet," Dad explained to Clara. "Come to that, so am I."

"You're not about to get another wild horse out there, are you?" Clara asked.

"Not so long as I'm livin' there," Dad muttered.

Sam smothered her smile. She loved wild horses and she was lucky enough to count several of them as friends. Ace and Popcorn, Dark Sunshine, and the mighty silver stallion known as the Phantom paraded through her imagination.

But Dad was a cattle rancher. He didn't like sharing the range with the mustangs. Still, Dad had a horseman's heart and sometimes he helped wild horses in spite of himself.

"No new mustangs," Sam told Clara as she gave Dad a serious nod. "But two new HARP girls are arriving today. Brynna's picking them up at the airport right now."

"What's HARP mean, again?" Clara asked.

Sam was a little surprised at Clara's interest. She looked up at the woman's face, framed by a pink scarf knotted around her hair. Two ends stuck up like rabbit's ears, adding to Clara's alert expression.

Ice clinked as Clara poured water into their glasses.

"The Horse and Rider Protection program," Sam explained.

"That's right. For bad girls and bad horses," Clara mused. She looked toward the back of her coffee shop, nodding.

"Well now," Dad said. "Not exactly bad. Just troubled, I guess."

Brynna called the girls "at risk," but Dad was being pretty generous in his description. After all, Mikki, the first HARP girl they'd had at the ranch, had set his barn on fire before she started changing her ways.

But Mikki had changed, and so had Popcorn. Both had become more trusting of people. That's what made Sam excited about this summer.

"I'm not saying there's anything wrong with it," Clara assured Dad. "In fact, I was thinking about making a donation."

The bell over the coffee shop's front door jingled. When she saw two new customers walk in, Clara stepped back from their table.

"Millie is late again," Clara muttered, looking around for the dark-haired waitress who usually helped out. "So I need to go wait on these folks, but I'll be back."

As Clara hurried off to seat her customers, Dad looked after her.

"Sure hope the donation's a cake or pie," he grumbled.

Or horse? Sam wondered.

Her pulse beat a little faster. Across the parking lot, Clara's coffee shop faced Phil's Fill-Up, a gas station and general store, but on the other side, acres of pastureland stretched toward Darton.

The fenced land belonged to a horse-loving banker, and though Sam hadn't noticed any new horses, it was possible she'd missed one.

Sam waited until Dad had taken a bite of his cheeseburger, then asked, "I wonder if Clara knows the HARP horses have to be mustangs?" Then she casually popped a French fry into her mouth.

"Honey, she's not about to be givin' us a horse. She couldn't afford to if she had one." Dad chewed and nodded. "Which she doesn't."

Just the same, he watched Clara as if she were a time bomb.

Sam started eating her own delicious lunch. Even though Gram made great home-cooked meals, Sam missed going out to eat. When she'd lived in San Francisco with Aunt Sue, they'd had about half their meals in restaurants. Although Clara's lacked a big city atmosphere, it was still a treat.

And a surprise.

Sam had expected Dad to drive straight home after they'd delivered Buff, a River Bend horse, to a lady in Darton who rented him each summer for her visiting grandchildren. Instead, Dad had pulled the truck and empty horse trailer into the parking lot between Clara's and Phil's Fill-Up.

Pulling on the parking brake, he'd declared that as long as they needed chicken feed from the Alkali store, they might as well have lunch, too.

But now Dad was watching the clock.

No surprise there, Sam thought. Dad couldn't forget the work awaiting him at home. Besides, Brynna would arrive at River Bend Ranch with the two new HARP girls pretty soon.

Sam had promised herself she'd be tolerant and understanding, no matter what kind of trouble the girls had been in. At River Bend Ranch, their pasts wouldn't matter.

She was feeling quite mature as she sipped her milk shake.

I'll treat them just like I'd want to be treated, Sam thought, but then her tranquility wavered. Dad put down his cheeseburger and his expression turned serious.

"About that chicken feed," he reminded her.

Sam knew he wasn't talking about the burlap bags of feed they'd just loaded into the truck.

"Dad, I didn't spill it," Sam insisted.

"Well, it wasn't much. You might not have noticed."

Sam sighed. There was no use contradicting him. Since she was the one in charge of feeding the Rhode

Island Red hens each morning, Dad was certain she was to blame for the grains of cracked corn he'd found on the tack room floor.

She let him talk, even though she didn't see why it was such a big deal. Her expression must have given her away.

"Samantha, this is important. Scattered grain attracts mice. Mice bring snakes. I hear this is gonna be a bad year for rattlers and I don't want anyone— two-legged or four—bein' bit."

"Okay," Sam agreed. The cheeseburger felt heavy in her stomach. Her arms crawled with chills.

"No need to look scared," Dad said. "Mostly they keep to themselves if you just leave them be."

Mostly?

"Okay," Sam said again. She wished she could keep the scared sound out of her voice.

She had nothing against snakes. She thought they were kind of interesting, but the two years she'd spent away from the ranch in San Francisco had done more than expose her to neat restaurants. She'd become nervous over things most ranch girls took for granted.

Like snakes.

"I'll be really careful," Sam promised.

She felt relieved as Millie rushed in through the restaurant's back door. Still trying to tie her apron strings, the tardy waitress attracted Dad's attention for a minute.

Then Clara crossed the coffee shop, wagging her order pad with raised eyebrows as she approached their table.

"Now," Clara said. "Before my lunch rush hits—"

Sam glanced out the front window. She could see the empty highway and the edge of the bone-white *playa*. Far out, blurred by heat waves, the Calico Mountains zigzagged against the blue Nevada sky. She couldn't imagine where a rush of lunch-hour diners would come from.

"I was joking, Sam," Clara said. "Afraid there's no lunch rush. If business doesn't pick up . . ." She gave a pained smile, then made a dismissing wave. "Anyway, I've got to tell you about this horse."

Dad placed the last of his burger on his plate and stared at it as if he'd lost his appetite.

"Oh now, Wyatt Forster, don't you go looking all mournful," Clara scolded him. "You're from a horse family and you went and married a horse-loving woman just last Christmas, so what do you expect?"

Dad leaned back in his chair with a tolerant smile.

"Go on, then," he told her.

"A man came in here yesterday for his lunch— about your age and occupation, I'd say—and while he was eating, I heard all kinds of racket outside. I remarked on it to him and it turned out he had a horse, a 'grew-ya gelding' he called him, that was goin' crazy."

Sam's mind spun as she tried to remember exactly

what a grulla-colored horse looked like.

"Goin' crazy?" Dad repeated. He chuckled, rubbed his forehead, and gave Sam a wry look as if he'd given up expecting normal horses.

"Not really *loco*," Clara explained. "It turns out, the gelding had been kicking the trailer all through Darton, and hadn't settled down yet. Well, to make a long story short, that cowboy, whose name is Henry Fox, of all things, told me that Jinx—that's the horse's name, poor fella—is just kinda rough around the edges like one of these delinquents. And he's a mustang."

Clara paused to meet Sam's eyes.

"Really?" Sam said.

"Really." Clara gave a nod. "He figured maybe the horse was from around here and got restless when he smelled the sage and sand of home. Anyway, this Henry Fox was hauling Jinx up to a ranch in Montana. 'It's the bronc's last chance,' is what he told me, 'cause this horse is just a natural born bad luck charm."

"That's silly," Sam said.

"Exactly." Clara pointed her index finger at Sam as if she'd guessed a correct answer. "That's just what I told him. And that's when he offered to sell Jinx to me for one dollar and a piece of pineapple upside-down cake."

A dollar and a piece of cake?

"Can I see him?" Sam asked, but Dad's voice was louder.

"What do you know about him?" Dad asked Clara. "You didn't get yourself stuck with some sick old nag, did you?"

"Wyatt," Clara scolded. "I'll tell you this, even though I don't have an eye for horseflesh, I am a pretty good businesswoman."

"Of course you are," Dad began.

"Besides, on the bill of sale, that cowboy, Henry, wrote down the phone number of the ranch in Montana, in case I wanted to call and ask him anything."

Dad shrugged casually, but Sam thought he looked eager to get going.

"Right away," Clara continued, "I had an idea of what to do with that horse." Clara had barely taken a breath before she seemed to veer to another topic. "Sam, are you in YRA?"

Sam shook her head. She'd heard of Young Ranchers of America. It was a local group modeled on Future Farmers of America, but she didn't know any kids who belonged.

"Well, they're having a fun day next weekend," Clara said, then darted across the coffee shop and peeled off the tape holding a flier to the glass pie case. When she returned and handed it to Sam, she added, "One of the things they're doing is having a claiming race."

Sam was trying to remember what happened in a claiming race.

"Sounds like a good idea," Dad said. He stood and pulled some dollar bills from his pocket, looking relieved, but Sam wasn't sure Clara had finished explaining her plan for the horse named Jinx.

"Jinx is right out back," Clara began, picking up their plates. "You can—"

Before she could finish her sentence, Phil, the owner of the gas station next door, burst into the coffee shop so fast that the welcoming bell's delicate tinkle was a clash.

"Clara, that horse is loose!"

Brakes squealed outside. Sam ran to the front window in time to see a horse dash past the back bumper of Dad's parked truck.

Smoky gray and determined, the horse shied at a blowing piece of newspaper. Would he turn back?

No. Hooves clattering, the horse galloped past the coffee shop and down the highway, headed for Darton. His black mane stood up like a Mohawk haircut. His tail streamed, glossy and thick, behind him. He moved with a liquid speed Sam had only seen once before.

"Look at him run," Sam gasped.

No one heard her words over the blaring horn and the sickening clash of metal crushing metal as a green sedan slammed into the back of Dad's truck.

It was going to be a bad afternoon, Sam realized as she pushed away from the window.

Dad grabbed his Stetson and jammed it on. Sam

caught up with him as he hurried outside.

Summer heat hit her at the same time she saw Jake jump out of the driver's seat of his mother's car. The afternoon had turned from bad to rotten. Sam turned away from the accident. She stared after the sound of hooves hitting on hot asphalt.

The grulla gelding kept running. He didn't look back to see if the clamor of cars and people followed him. He didn't lunge into the sand for better traction.

Sam couldn't look away from the escaping horse.

Head and tail flung high, eyes set on his own goal, the grulla ran right down the dotted white line in the middle of the highway.

Chapter Two ๑

"Howdy, Jake," Dad drawled.

"Wyatt."

Jake only said Dad's name, but it sounded like an apology.

Jake stared at the spot where the green fender pressed against the blue one. He'd driven his mom's car into Dad's and not only was Dad his closest neighbor, he was often his boss.

Sam felt sorry for Jake, but someone needed to go after Jinx. Why were they all just standing here?

Even Clara. Though the grulla belonged to her, she seemed more interested in the accident.

"You tried to miss the horse," Dad guessed.

"Yeah. I would have if he hadn't shied. Still."

Jake sighed. "Maybe we should call the sheriff."

Sam gritted her teeth to keep from shouting that Jinx could be lost by then.

Sheriff Ballard would have to drive all the way from Darton. That would take at least half an hour.

"I know calling the sheriff is the right thing to do," Sam said. Jake glanced up as if he were just seeing her for the first time. "But Jinx is running down the highway, alone. You missed him, Jake, but someone else might not."

"Jinx," Jake echoed. One corner of his mouth quirked up. "Who's he belong to?"

"Me," Clara said. Her hands moved toward her tied apron strings, as if to take it off, but then she shook her head. "Maybe there's something to what that cowboy said, after all. Maybe that gelding earned his name, fair and square."

That was ridiculous, but Sam didn't want to get in trouble for correcting Clara, so she didn't say so.

"Someone still needs to go after him," she insisted.

"You're right," Clara agreed. "He's my responsibility. I can't have him running loose." Clara turned to Dad. "It's kind of adding insult to injury, and I hate to ask, Wyatt, but since you have that empty horse trailer, if your truck isn't hurt too bad . . ."

"It's just a dent," Dad said.

Thumb through one belt loop, he looked unconcerned, as if he didn't care that there was no extra money to fix his truck.

"If I'd turned the other direction, I mighta missed the truck *and* the horse," Jake said slowly. Sam could tell he was replaying the accident to figure out what he'd done wrong.

"Don't fret over it," Dad said.

Sam shifted from foot to foot. They had to hurry.

The accident couldn't be undone. Whoever was at fault would still be at fault later, but Jinx was galloping away. Now he was just a blur in the middle of the highway.

The desert looked flat, but it had dips and rises. Any minute, a car could crest a hill and the speeding driver would barely have time to see Jinx right in front of him.

"I'll stay here and wait for the sheriff. It's just a formality anyway," Dad said. He took the truck keys from his pocket. "You and Sam go get Clara's horse."

Jake's jaw was set hard. Sam couldn't tell what he was thinking as he took the keys. Jake didn't thank Dad for trusting him in spite of the crash. He just nodded.

And Dad didn't tell Jake to hurry. Even though Brynna was probably standing in the airport welcoming the HARP girls to Nevada right now and Dad wanted to be on his way home, helping a neighbor was more important.

"Jake, want me to call your mom?" Dad asked.

Jake swallowed so loudly that Sam heard him.

"I'd better do it," Jake said.

"You're a brave kid," Clara said. "Maxine sure likes that little Honda."

"I'll call when we get back," Jake said. Then, he moved toward the truck and Sam knew he was ready to go. She hurried to climb into her usual seat on the passenger's side.

"There's ropes and whatnot in there," Dad called after them. Jake waved out the window as the engine roared to life.

Jinx shone like steel under the summer sun.

"How should we do it, do you think?" Sam asked.

She looked sideways at Jake. She could tell he'd pushed the accident to the back of his mind. He was trying to think like a horse.

Jake drove at half speed, hanging back so he wouldn't spook Jinx. Not that they could sneak up on him while they were dragging the trailer.

Jake stayed alert for other traffic, but he appeared to be reading the gelding's body language.

"It's almost like he knows where he's goin'," Jake said, then his eyes narrowed. "Wish I coulda seen him clearly before this. Did you?"

If Jake was looking for a hint of the horse's temperament, Sam knew she'd be no help.

"No. We were having lunch and Clara was telling us she'd swapped a piece of pineapple upside-down cake for a horse."

The truck slowed suddenly. At first, Sam thought

Jake's foot had come off the accelerator in surprise. Then, she noticed he was steering off the right shoulder of the road.

Ahead, Jinx slackened his pace. He meandered from one side of the white line to the other. He moved at a rapid trot, ears flicking from side to side.

"He mighta lost his way," Jake said. "We can haze him off the road."

"He'd be safer from cars," Sam said. She sat up straighter, taking in the terrain around them. "We're not far from War Drum Flats."

A million years ago, War Drum Flats had been the bottom of a sea that had covered much of Nevada. Most of the lake had dried up, but it had left behind smooth footing that would be easier on the gelding's hooves. And Jinx might stop to drink at the remaining pond.

"We're also close to Lost Canyon," Jake said.

"We'll never catch him if he decides to go in there," Sam said.

Lost Canyon was honeycombed with sandy basins and steep trails, secret paths and dead ends.

The gelding glanced back over his sweat-sleek shoulder at them. His dark-shaded face and ears flashed annoyance. Then he jumped as if hurdling an invisible fence on the left side of the highway. Off the pavement, he broke into a gallop once more.

"There he goes," she said.

Heading back, Jinx would pass trails to Lost

Canyon and Arroyo Azul before crossing War Drum
Flats.

All of this was the Phantom's territory.

"If he runs into the Phantom, what do you think
will happen?" she asked Jake as he steered after the
running horse.

"You know that stud better than I do. Can't see
him bein' real friendly, though."

Sam agreed. Jinx was no threat to the Phantom's
kingship, but the grulla gelding was a stranger.
During the summer months, range stallions guarded
their herds jealously.

All at once the gelding's smooth speed reminded
Sam of the flier in her pocket.

"Hey, what's a claiming race?" she asked Jake.

"YRA's havin' one."

"I know, but what is it, exactly?" Sam asked.

"Pay a small entry fee to enter a horse in a race,"
Jake said in a tone that said she should know. "Then,
up until like, five minutes before the race, anyone can
claim him for a set fee. Like in a $1,000 claiming race,
you have your pick of horses for $1,000."

"Before the race," Sam mused. You'd have to have
solid faith in your own judgment to buy a horse that
way. "And do you want him to get claimed?"

"Do I want *who* to get claimed? I wouldn't enter
any of our horses."

"No," Sam said, but her mind darted to Clara.
"But why would you do it?"

"I wouldn't. Brat, what are you talking about?" Jake demanded, glancing away from the road.

"Never mind," Sam said. "How should we catch Jinx?"

As they rolled across the range after the horse, Jake didn't answer. Sam felt restless and anxious. "Or haven't you figured that out yet?"

Jake shrugged. "Take a close look up ahead."

Sam's eyes skimmed over the blue-green sage-brush and occasional black rocks until they spotted War Drum Flats. They showed on the horizon, smooth as a beige tablecloth except for the toy-sized horses at the edge of the pond.

For an instant, the mustangs were just streaks of color. Blood bay, black, sorrel, roan. Sam widened her eyes so she could see them more clearly. She leaned forward, straining against her seat belt. When the truck hit a bump, Jake's arm flashed out to bar her from banging her chin on the dashboard.

As she watched, the wild horses melted into a gully thick with pinion pine. One horse stayed behind. It was the Phantom.

Sam felt as if a bird fluttered where her heart belonged. Years ago, the Phantom had been hers and she'd seen him every day. Now, each sighting was a gift, a reward for living in this wild country.

"Looks like he's in prime condition," Jake said.

Sam didn't take her eyes from the stallion. Still,

she smiled. Sometimes it seemed as if Jake and the Phantom were enemies, but, like Dad, Jake was a horseman as well as a cattleman. He had to admire the splendid stallion.

"He's not paying much attention to Jinx," Sam said. "I can't figure that out."

The Phantom waited, lips lowered near the ground.

"He's watching," Jake said, amused. "He's pretending to graze, but he's luring the gelding close enough to get a good look."

Jake was right.

If the Phantom believed Jinx was set on stealing mares, he would have flexed his neck muscles in challenge.

Instead, the silver stallion moved with trancelike steps, acting as if he sought nothing more than a tender bite of grass.

"Do you think Jinx is fooled?" Sam asked.

Neck drawn back, ears pointed toward the Phantom, Jinx didn't look submissive. He continued toward the trampled area around the pond.

Would the Phantom let him drink?

"We'd better stop," Jake said, braking until the pickup halted. "If they think the truck's a threat, the stallion might let Jinx join the herd until danger's passed. My dad said he's seen two stallions do that — join forces against an enemy, sort of."

Sam wasn't so sure. The Phantom was always on the lookout for trouble, and she'd seen him fight other stallions. The battles had been vicious and bloody. She couldn't believe he'd let another male mingle with his mares.

"Watch out," she blurted as the Phantom raised his head, flattened his ears, then lunged, mouth open.

Jinx stopped, though the pale stallion had only advanced a few feet closer.

"I think," Sam said quietly, "he's just telling Jinx who's the boss around here."

"Maybe," Jake said.

Mane glinting like tinsel, the Phantom trotted forward.

Jinx looked away, swishing his black tail in apparent boredom, though Sam would bet he was still watching the stallion from the corner of his eye.

Why didn't Jinx retreat? That's all it would take to satisfy the stallion.

When Jinx held his ground, the Phantom lowered his head into a herding position. His shoulder muscles bunched as he advanced. The gelding sidestepped, eyes rolling.

Suddenly aware that Jake was rummaging around in the truck, Sam pried her gaze from the horses.

"What are you doing?" she asked.

"Getting out. Your horse is gonna drive that gelding back this way. When he does, I'll rope him."

"I'm coming with you," Sam said, but the truck door had just closed when the Phantom charged.

Chapter Three ↷

$\mathcal{I}$t turned out Jake was wrong. Instead of coming toward them, Jinx ran after the mares. They'd passed through the gully. Now they stood on the ridge line, flicking their tails as they gazed down at the excitement below.

A short neigh of rage burst from the Phantom as he lunged after the gelding.

Hearing the stallion's hooves closing on him, Jinx increased his speed.

"He can run," Jake said.

Gusts of wind might have blown at his heels, keeping him half a length ahead of the Phantom.

A stranger would have taken Jinx for the horse who'd spent the winter in the wild. His grulla coat was dull and patchy, his movements rough.

The silver stallion shone in the sun. Living off the land, searching out each mouthful of food had made him sleek, lean, and strong. He moved with a tireless grace.

Still, Sam admitted, each time the Phantom put on a burst of speed, Jinx surged ahead.

"Why would a man give away a horse that can run like that?" Jake asked.

"I can't believe it," she whispered. "The Phantom's got to catch him."

Jinx no longer chased after the mares. He flew across the *playa*, wheeling right when the Phantom tried to nip his neck. Then he rushed left when the frustrated stallion circled to the other side, trying to ram his mighty shoulder against the gelding's, to shove him off balance.

Branches cracked as the horses trampled a clump of sagebrush in their path. The herbal smell blew to Sam on a hot wind.

"When are they going to stop?" she asked.

"It's a grudge match, now, but the gelding didn't drink," Jake pointed out. "He'll slow down soon."

And then what? Sam wondered.

Even though they were still half a mile away, she heard the horses' breathing. Their speed said they weren't exhausted, but they were working hard.

Which horse would win? A tangle of loyalty and sympathy wouldn't let Sam take sides.

And then, she didn't have to.

Through a secret set of signals, the horses agreed to stop. Half-rearing, the Phantom rose above the gelding, pawing with his front hooves. He didn't touch the grulla, but he left no question about his dominance.

Jinx backed toward the pond, watching the stallion return to all fours. He stared after the Phantom as the pale horse trotted back to his herd.

"Wow." Sam felt air whoosh through her lips as if she'd been holding her breath.

Beside her, Jake tightened his grip on the coiled rope in his left hand. He turned his right hand, rolling his wrist, loosening it up for a throw. As he took a step toward the horse, he gave Sam a look that said *stay back*.

She didn't argue. Jinx wasn't acting too spooked now, but he'd proven he'd be tough to catch if he decided to run. It only made sense for her to stay at the truck, blending in, while Jake roped him.

Jake held the lariat against his leg as he sauntered toward the pond. If the horse had ever been roped before, he wouldn't be fooled.

The grulla drank noisily. In the instant he raised his dripping muzzle, Jake sent a loop to settle gently over the horse's head.

Jinx snorted and Jake stood still as the horse backed splashing into the pond. When he reached the end of it, the rope tightened about halfway down the grulla's neck, pressing a flat spot in his Mohawk mane.

Jake made a clucking noise. The gelding released a sigh that shook his entire body and then, when Jake turned to walk back toward the trailer, he followed.

Sam unfurled her fingers, which had been gripped into fists. She hurried to open the trailer so that Jake could load the horse without a lot of commotion.

Then she looked back at the approaching pair.

When she'd been a kid, working with the black colt that had grown up to be the Phantom, Jake had told her it was always easier to get a horse to do what you wanted him to do if the horse thought it was his own idea.

The grulla was tired. He'd probably like a ride back home—wherever that turned out to be—and so he followed Jake.

As the horse came closer, walking in step with Jake, Sam finally got a good look at him.

Running, he'd been beautiful. Now, he looked neglected.

"Think I'd call him Orphan, not Jinx," Jake muttered as he stopped just short of the open trailer.

"Wouldn't you love to see what's under that clumpy dead hair?" Sam asked.

Jake didn't look intrigued. His expression said he wasn't as fond of currying as he was cowboying.

It was almost as if Jinx wore a ragged disguise,

Sam thought. The gelding was still shedding his winter coat. Beneath it, just waiting to be exposed by a shedding blade and curry comb, Sam glimpsed hair that looked silvery tan, with a shimmer of blue mixed in. That undercoat had shone like metal as he ran.

Jake let the rope fall slack between his hands and the horse's neck when the grulla extended a dark muzzle toward the trailer and gave a questioning sniff.

Jinx's ears and face, legs and shoulders were smudged with a dark chocolate shade that showed up again on his dorsal stripe. About as wide as Sam's thumb was long, the stripe flowed from the end of his mane to the base of his full, black tail.

Jinx stood about fifteen hands tall. The BLM freeze brand on his neck was impossible to read under all that hair, but the brand on his left shoulder was clear.

"I guess that's supposed to be a heart," Sam said.

Jake nodded, and touched the scar. The horse twitched, but he didn't pull away.

"I'm about to remember whose brand it is," Jake said. "He musta jumped when they set that iron on his hide." Jake's index finger traced the gaps in the symbol.

Sam brushed her bangs back from her eyes and mentally ordered herself to get a grip.

It was only the horse's resigned attitude that made her think the brand looked like a broken heart.

* * *

At first they thought Jinx would load easily. Watchful but quiet, he seemed reconciled to moving on. Sam and Jake both thought so.

When Sam begged Jake to let her take over, he agreed.

"Fine," he said, handing her the rope. "I need to fix somethin'."

"Hey, pretty boy," Sam crooned to Jinx. When the gelding's ears flicked in interest, Sam looked over at Jake for approval.

But Jake was sitting in the driver's seat of the truck, taking off a shoe. Before now, she hadn't noticed he wasn't wearing boots. He shook the shoe as if he'd gotten a pebble in it.

As she led Jinx toward the trailer, Sam cast around in her mind for some way to tease Jake, and that's when the gelding balked.

The rope tightened between them.

"Come on, now," Sam encouraged the horse. When he didn't budge, she tightened her hands on the rope and gave it a yank.

She didn't want Jinx to think he could get the best of her.

The gelding laid his ears flat against his neck, then jerked his head skyward. She could only see his throat. Her arms straightened until she thought they'd pop from her sockets.

"I think that bronc is about to show you what he's made of," Jake muttered.

Jake didn't sound worried, but that was no comfort to Sam. If Jake's hat were on fire, he'd just mumble something about it being warm.

Jinx began backing away. Sam couldn't stop him, even though she'd spread her boots apart and lowered her weight. Her bootheels were probably leaving furrows in the earth.

Suddenly her memory replayed Dad's voice saying that when a horse was as mean as Witch, Jake's mare, the only safe place was on her back.

"Do you want to try to mount him?" Sam asked.

"Are you crazy?"

Okay, so that was a bad idea, Sam thought as the horse towed her a few inches farther from the trailer.

Made bold by the fact that he was winning, Jinx shook his head and started to bolt. His hooves scattered dust and he stared toward the highway that led to Darton.

"Hey, I don't know what you lost down that road, but you're not going after it," Sam scolded him.

When his ears flicked in her direction, she rushed closer to him, going hand over hand down the rope, tightening it around Jinx's neck until she'd wedged her shoulder against his.

The smoke-brown face swung around so fast, Sam couldn't have escaped if he'd meant to whack her with his muzzle. But he didn't.

Jinx could take a bite of her face right now if he wanted to. Sam swallowed and tried more sweet talk.

"Hey, good boy, I didn't mean to hurt your feelings."

Jinx stared at her with big brown eyes, then pressed his brow against hers.

"I just meant you're not going down that road today," she whispered. "Maybe later."

He was so close she couldn't focus. She smelled his hot hide and felt the prickly, growing-out forelock against her bangs.

Jinx gave a hay-scented snort, then backed up a step. As soon as the pressure on Sam's face was relieved, the rope was snatched from her hand.

It was only Jake, taking over as usual. She let him, because she needed a minute to think.

Sam's arms curled around her ribs. Something had happened between her and the grulla. She wasn't sure what.

She tried to figure it out as Jinx went willingly into the trailer. His hooves shifted around, striking the floor, but he was only settling in.

Jake locked the latch and turned toward her.

"Of all the fool things I've seen you do . . . ," he began slowly.

"It worked," Sam said. "You can't argue with that."

"Don't plan to."

"Here's what I was thinking," Sam began, though Jake hadn't asked. "You know how when you walk behind a horse, you get close enough that they can't get up enough momentum to kick you hard?"

It didn't matter that Jake stared off toward the hillside, ignoring her. She kept talking. "Well, I just did it from the other end."

Jake rubbed the back of his neck and gave a snort almost as loud as Jinx's.

"There are so many things wrong with—" Jake broke off and started over. "The leverage alone, not to mention the logic—"

"But it did work," Sam interrupted.

"Yeah," Jake said, as she started back toward the driver's seat of the truck. "But it shouldn't have."

That sure didn't feel like a victory, Sam thought. But it was as close as she'd get to one. She hesitated before getting back into the truck and it was then she spotted a swirl of dust halfway up the ridge.

The Phantom's mares had disappeared, but there in the thicket clogging the gully, staring through wind-tortured pinion pines, stood the silver stallion.

Jinx must have sensed the stallion, because his neigh echoed from inside the trailer and it rocked with his weight.

Was the Phantom just keeping watch? Two humans, their truck, and the pushy gelding constituted a disturbance in the Phantom's day. Maybe he was just making sure they didn't change their minds and come after his mares.

But Sam didn't think that was it.

She knew the Phantom. He was the most dominant stallion on this range, but the grulla gelding had nearly outrun him.

Could the Phantom be sending Jinx a silent promise that their rivalry wasn't over?

You'll see me again, she imagined the stallion saying.

The white blur beyond the pinions pines grew hazy, then vanished.

Chapter Four ❧

Sheriff Ballard had arrived by the time Sam and Jake drove up to Clara's coffee shop and parked Dad's truck and the horse trailer.

Sam saw Jake's hands tighten on the steering wheel. Why did the sight of the sheriff's black-and-white car make him nervous?

The minute she spotted Sheriff Ballard in his khaki uniform, Sam felt relieved. She liked the gruff, by-the-book police officer.

A few weeks earlier, just before school was out, he'd helped her understand the circumstances of her mother's death. After years of being kept in the dark, she'd appreciated being treated like an adult. Besides, she liked his droopy mustache because it reminded her of an Old West lawman in a movie.

Carefully, Jake put on the emergency brake and turned the truck's key to OFF.

"Wonder if anyone's called my mom," Jake said quietly.

So it wasn't the sheriff making Jake nervous, Sam thought. He was worried over what his mom would say about the damage to her car. Sam didn't blame him. Jake had the same kind of family she did. Mistakes had big-time consequences.

"She'll understand, won't she?" Sam asked. "After all, you're a good driver. You were only trying to keep from hitting Jinx."

Jake picked up his black Stetson from its place on the seat between them.

"Hope she sees it that way," he said.

Together they climbed down from the truck and side by side approached the spot where Clara, Dad, and Sheriff Ballard had gathered.

The sheriff greeted them with a grim expression. It wasn't a frown and he didn't look angry, just very serious.

"Jake, I expect you know you're not supposed to leave the scene of an accident."

Sam didn't know Jake had stopped until she'd walked a few steps beyond him.

Looking back over her shoulder, she saw he'd been about to position his Stetson on his blue-black hair when the sheriff spoke. Jake's hand stopped halfway to his head, then he let it drop to his side, still holding the hat.

"Yeah," he said.

"I—"

"We—"

Together, Dad and Clara explained they'd asked Jake to take the truck and trailer after the runaway horse.

Sam wondered if she'd be able to memorize all the rules of the road so that she could get a driver's license when she was sixteen.

It made sense that you didn't move cars that had been in an accident. Their positions might help the sheriff decide who was to blame. And yet all these adult drivers had encouraged Jake to do just that.

"All the same, it could be considered a hit-and-run," Sheriff Ballard said.

Hit and run. Sam's breath caught in her chest. She knew that was serious.

It grew so quiet she heard a ding as a car pulled up to the gas pumps at Phil's Fill-Up. She heard a car door slam and coins tinkle into a slot before a soda can rattled out of a vending machine. Still, no one moved.

"It wasn't a hit-and-run," Sam protested. "He stopped and talked with everyone—"

Sheriff Ballard held up a calming hand. "I know that, but in some places, it might not matter. It's not a good habit to get into." His chin lifted and he met

Jake's eyes, waiting for a response.

"No sir," Jake agreed. Just above his faded yellow shirt, Jake's throat moved as he swallowed. "Thanks for the warning. I'll remember."

"Now, since this accident happened on private property"—Sheriff Ballard's nod took in the parking lot—"and there's no one hurt or any signs of substance abuse, it's of no interest to the county."

A shuddery breath made its way through Sam's lips. She noticed Dad look down, shaking his head in relief, and decided she'd just discovered another reason to love him. Dad was more worried about Jake than he was his own truck.

"I'll write up an accident report for your insurance company, Jake. Hope it does you some good."

"Thanks," Jake said, but Sam could tell by the way his jaw stayed set in a hard, smooth line, that Jake dreaded facing his mother.

"Now, tell me about the horse," Sheriff Ballard said.

Jake's attention turned inward for a minute, as if he were replaying what they'd seen out on the range.

"He might be the fastest horse I've ever seen," Jake said.

"Is that so?" Sheriff Ballard's voice lifted as he glanced toward the trailer.

"The cowboy who sold him to me said he was 'frightenin' fast,' that he could throw dirt in the eyes of a jackrabbit," Clara said. "But I chalked it up to exaggeration. Besides, where are you going to race a fast mustang?" she asked, looking a little sly. "Not against Thoroughbreds or Quarter Horses."

"He *is* fast," Sam admitted, thinking of the flier tucked in her pocket.

"Sometime I'd like to take a look at him," said Sheriff Ballard.

"You in the market for a horse?" Dad asked, surprised.

"Could be." The sheriff tapped the end of his pen against the unopened pad of citations he held. "A horse would be handy for search and rescue situations, but let's finish this up. What do you say?"

A half an hour later, Sheriff Ballard's patrol car pulled away.

"The dent's nothing," Dad told Jake as he apologized once more. "This old truck has a dozen more just like it."

Jake nodded his appreciation for Wyatt's acceptance. Then, with the grim determination of a guy on his way to his own hanging, Jake left, too.

Dad started toward the rear of the horse trailer to unload Jinx.

"I want you to keep him," Clara blurted.

Sam caught her breath and held it as Dad turned to face Clara.

Before he could protest, Clara said, "Probably you're thinking you don't need another mouth to feed on River Bend Ranch, but he's a mustang. You can tell by that light spot on his neck, even if you can't quite read the brand."

"Saw it."

"And if that HARP program would pay his room and board . . ." Clara let her voice trail off.

"I don't think so," Dad said, but he looked uneasy.

Dad's habit of being neighborly had him in a quandary, Sam thought. River Bend Ranch didn't need another horse, but Clara's request sounded temporary. Dad probably didn't want to offend Clara over the cost of a few scoops of oats.

"Since he's real nimble-footed," Clara sighed, then interrupted her own careful negotiating. "Oh shoot, Wyatt. I want to run him in that YRA claiming race. I might make a little extra money.

"Maybe you could take the rough edges off him before the race and Sam could ride him. We could share the profits."

"Dad?" Sam knew better than to get into the discussion, but she couldn't stop herself.

"Go on, you might as well put in your two cents worth," Dad told her.

"Brynna said she thought we'd be using Popcorn and Dark Sunshine to work with the new girls. They're the only two horses that really belong to HARP, and since Tempest has just been born—"

"That buckskin's even more cantankerous than before," Dad said.

He still didn't trust Dark Sunshine, and Sam didn't blame him. She'd stood watch as the abused buckskin had given birth to the beautiful black filly she'd named Tempest, but she didn't think a stranger would be safe around the mustang mare.

"We've got Ace," Dad said. "And Penny. They were both wild."

Sam shifted her weight. She knew what she wanted to say, but she didn't want to sound sappy. Finally, she just blurted it out.

"Neither of them needs a second chance. Jinx does."

Dad shook his head. "Sorry, ladies. No sale."

When Dad shot back the bolt holding the trailer doors closed, Jinx startled and jumped forward. As the doors opened, the horse gazed over his shoulder with troubled eyes.

Sam thought of the broken heart brand the gelding wore. Jinx might not bring bad luck, but he sure had his share of it.

"I can't blame you, Wyatt," Clara said. "Just the same, Sam, you might take a look at the flier. Here, let me put my phone number on it." Clara fished a pen from her pocket, took the flier from Sam, then handed it back.

After a moment of uneasy silence, Clara shaded her eyes to look down the highway.

"Isn't that Grace's car?" Clara asked.

"Yep," Dad said, recognizing Gram's yellow

Buick. "Brynna took it to pick up the HARP girls."

As the car slowed, Sam felt a fizzing combination of excitement and dread. It was going to be cool to be sort of a camp counselor for the two girls, but what kind of problems would they bring with them?

Slowly and quietly, Dad closed the trailer doors again, but his gesture said it was just temporary.

It might not be, Sam thought. Maybe there'd be an extra girl in the car. Maybe they'd need another horse. Sam crossed her fingers. Maybe Jinx's luck was about to change.

Dust still swirled as Brynna climbed out of the yellow car. She wore a bright summer dress, but her smile was strained.

"What is it?" Dad asked. He seemed to cover the yards between himself and Brynna in one long stride.

Looking both pleased and embarrassed, Brynna waved Dad away. "Nothing, really," she said.

"Tell us," Sam said, hurrying closer.

"You two," Brynna laughed, shaking her head. "All your fussing is embarrassing. Now I see how silly I'm being."

The screen door to the cafe closed quietly as Clara went back inside, leaving the three Forsters alone.

"One of the girls is going to be a handful," Brynna told them.

"You expected that," Dad said.

Brynna matched her fingertips together before she added, "It's Crystal. She missed her plane and we had to wait for her. Luckily, the second plane was only an hour behind the first, but she didn't offer anything like an apology."

Sam waited. That couldn't be all.

"We only have one week to make a difference in these girls' lives and she missed her plane." Brynna stood stiff.

"Well, yeah," Dad said.

Brynna had a college degree in biology. Her logical, scientific mind had made her director of Willow Springs Wild Horse Center. She didn't get angry very often, and yet she seemed on the verge of it already.

Sam's thoughts flew to the horses. If the girl was inconsiderate of people, how would she be with the mustangs?

In the HARP program, a horse "belonged" to each girl for the entire week. Would Brynna let this Crystal have sweet, wise Popcorn?

She couldn't trust her with Penny, could she? Even though the sorrel mustang had lots of spirit, blindness made her vulnerable.

Sam took a deep breath and reminded herself she'd decided to like these girls.

A hoof crashed against the metal trailer. Could Jinx be reacting to the tension whirling around out here?

"I thought you were taking Buff in early," Brynna said.

"We did," Dad told her. "That's Clara's horse."

"Clara's?" Brynna asked.

"She just got him. She bought him for a dollar and a piece of upside-down cake," Sam said, knowing Brynna couldn't resist such a story. "He's a mustang and—"

"*And*, we're about to unload him," Dad insisted.

"Unless we want to use him for the HARP program," Sam hurried on. She didn't look at Dad. "Clara said we could."

Brynna's eyes narrowed in thought, then she was moving to peek into the back of the trailer. She peered through the side. Finally, she moved to the front.

Dad didn't say a word, just sighed as if the argument were already lost.

"What's he like?" Brynna asked.

"He likes goin' back inside that pasture and never seein' us again," Dad insisted.

When Brynna shook her head so that her red braid flopped over her shoulder, she looked much cheerier.

"I mean, what's his temperament? Is he dangerous? Sam?"

"His name is Jinx and he's a little feisty, but he doesn't act mean," she said honestly.

This didn't seem like a good time to bring up his speed, or the claiming race. Despite Dad's pessimism, wasn't it possible that HARP could buy him for more than Clara would get in the claiming race?

"Don't forget that part where he brings bad luck wherever he goes," Dad muttered.

Together, Sam and Brynna stared at him in amazement.

"Not that I believe it," Dad added.

"How do you think he'd react to a ham-fisted rider?" Brynna asked.

Sam's mind replayed the moment she'd tried to force Jinx to do what she wanted. He'd almost jerked her off her feet. When she'd been sweet to him, he'd done as she asked.

"If you're nice to him, he's nice to you," Sam diagnosed.

"Perfect." Brynna nodded with satisfaction. "Wyatt, I promise I'll find a way to pay for his feed. Just please," she said, putting her hand on Dad's sleeve, "please take that horse to our house."

Chapter Five ∽

When Dad's truck and the horse trailer rumbled over the wooden bridge spanning the La Charla River and under the high wooden rectangle marking the ranch entrance, River Bend looked like it always did.

The two-story white house stood on the right. A grassy pasture spread over ten acres on the left and a scatter of corrals covered the area between the bridge and the barn.

But things weren't normal. The hens were nowhere in sight. The horses in the ten-acre pasture raced along the fence, anxious and excited. Blaze, the ranch's watchdog, stood barking in the middle of the ranch yard.

The HARP girls had already disrupted life at River Bend.

"Shall I put Jinx in the pasture?" Sam asked.

"I'll take care of that," Dad said. "You'd best go meet the girls."

"I'd rather take care of Jinx," Sam sighed. "Horses are easier."

Dad turned the truck key off. When he turned to her, his sun-browned face creased into a smile.

"Don't blame you," he said. "But you signed on to wrangle the humans."

"I know," Sam moaned. "Brynna told me about them last night, and I didn't really think they'd be so bad. But if they've got her worried already, I don't know if I have a chance."

"I'm not sure she should have told you all that was a good idea," Dad said. "You mighta formed decent opinions of these girls. Mikki turned out all right."

"I can hardly wait to see her," Sam agreed.

Mikki Short, the first HARP girl, had started out rough and impatient, but she'd ended up helping Popcorn make the transition from a frightened horse to a trusting one.

As a reward for passing her middle school classes and making up the credits she'd lost when she was in trouble, HARP was bringing Mikki back later this summer as a counselor's assistant, to work with Sam.

Both of these new girls could turn around just the way Mikki had, right?

"Brynna said it was safer for her to tell me a few things about each of the girls," Sam said, when neither she nor Dad made a move to get out of the truck. "And we're supposed to have 'breakfast meetings' and exchange information every morning before the girls get up."

"Sounds like gossip to me," Dad said.

Sam sort of agreed, but Brynna was the teacher. Brynna wanted Jake to be her co-teacher so he could take over when she returned to work at Willow Springs Wild Horse Center, but Jake had declined.

Despite the salary HARP offered, Jake didn't think he was cut out for teaching.

So, Sam would act as Brynna's student teacher by day, and at night, she'd sleep in the bunkhouse with the girls.

"She didn't tell me a bunch of personal details," Sam said. "Just that Crystal's dad works in a casino in Las Vegas and she's been in a lot of trouble since her mom died. I guess she's done crazy stuff like jumping off a roof into the school swimming pool and stealing a car to go joyriding."

Sam had found that hard to believe, since both girls had just finished seventh grade.

"Guess I'll be takin' my keys up to bed with me." Dad said it like a joke, but Sam knew he'd do just that.

"And Emily—" she began. "I mean, *Amelia*, is a total follower, and that's what gets her into trouble."

Big trouble, Sam thought. Brynna had mentioned that even in her small town in New Mexico, Amelia had been accused of shoplifting, cutting class, and alcohol abuse.

Dad rubbed his rough palms together. "Sounds like one heck of a long week to me, honey. How about you?"

It sounded like forever, especially when Sam thought of trying to do her usual chores, too.

Still, sappy as it would sound if she tried to explain, Sam knew she'd been lucky. She hadn't done anything to deserve her loving family. If she'd been born into Mikki's family, or Crystal's or Amelia's, life might have been different. She would probably be different.

A little embarrassed by her own corny thoughts, she rolled her eyes in mock horror.

"Tell me why we're doing this, again?" she joked, but Dad answered seriously.

"Helping horses and kids is Brynna's dream," Dad said. "If she's willing to take vacation time to do this, how can I say no? And we can use that HARP money."

As she opened the truck door to climb down, Sam's eyes were already searching the barn corral, looking for the tiny black filly. Sam wanted to take this last, unscheduled moment to check on Dark Sunshine and Tempest.

She'd only taken a few steps when the bunkhouse door opened and Brynna came out with two girls.

They were so quiet. Sam heard nothing but the crunch of dirt beneath their shoes. It was weird. Without knowing it, Sam had grown to expect lively conversation and laughter any time three people were together on this ranch.

A girl walked on each side of Brynna. The dark-haired one was pretty. She held her shoulders stiffly, but her head swiveled from side to side as if she couldn't believe she didn't see anyone she knew.

The other girl's fine, light-brown hair was almost invisible. She wore thick-lensed glasses with dark-red frames. Even from a distance, Sam noticed she was pale. She, too, looked around the ranch, but her steps were choppy. She held her hands in front of her, not clasped, but tumbling over and over each other, like mice on a wheel.

Although Sam longed to visit Tempest, she walked out to meet the girls.

"Sam!" Brynna beckoned her closer. "Come meet Amelia and Crystal. Girls, this is my daughter Samantha."

My *daughter*. Not stepdaughter. Sam smiled at Brynna, but she felt a little shy as she extended her hand toward Crystal.

The girl's hand closed around hers, warm and soft. Crystal's springy black hair fell to her shoulders and though she matched Sam in height, she seemed taller. She assessed Sam with ice-blue eyes that fixed on her work-scarred boots and the brown Stetson she held.

When Crystal released her hand, Sam started to brush off the dusty Western hat.

"Nice to meet you." Crystal had a weird way of giving the same emphasis to each word. It made her sound bored.

Amelia's stance changed after Crystal's words and her interested expression disappeared. She fumbled a cell phone from her pocket.

Why? Sam wondered. She hadn't heard it ring.

When Brynna cleared her throat, Amelia shoved the phone back in her pocket and reached out to shake Sam's hand.

It wasn't much of a greeting. Amelia gave Sam's hand a single downward tug, then pulled her cold palm out of reach. As she did, Sam noticed a blue tracery of veins showed in the girl's hands and near her hairline.

Don't stare, Sam told herself, then she asked, "Have you met the horses yet?"

"They haven't come over for an introduction," Crystal said, sarcastically. "Only you."

"Yeah," Amelia echoed.

If she'd been meeting them at school, Sam would have waved and walked away. But this wasn't school.

Sam looked to Brynna for help.

"I'll select your horses," Brynna said, "once I get to know each of you better."

As Brynna walked toward the ten-acre pasture, the two girls lagged behind.

Because she was a few yards ahead, Brynna probably didn't hear Crystal whisper, "Who cares?"

"You should," Sam said, making sure she sounded mature, not rude. "The horse will be yours all week. If it's a good match, you'll have more fun."

Crystal's pale eyes didn't change, but her lips gave a phony smile. "This isn't a vacation for us, you know."

"Yeah," Amelia said. "You're supposed to help us get our heads straight."

"Not me," Sam said. "The horses do that."

If you'll let them, she added silently.

Crystal shrugged. Amelia copied her, but Sam noticed Amelia's gaze had strayed ahead to the pasture.

"As you know," Brynna said once they all stood at the fence, "you'll be paired with a mustang. Most of these animals are saddle horses. See if you can guess which ones were born in the wild."

Dad had turned Jinx into the small pipe corral next to the pasture. They'd built it a few weeks ago to help introduce Penny into the saddle herd.

Now Jinx stood alone, watching the other horses as they checked him out, feinting kicks and snapping teeth in his direction.

Sam sighed. Horses made a very big deal of establishing dominance. For some reason, a chunky roan mare named Strawberry ranked highest. She ate first, crowded other horses away from the water trough, and constantly reminded the rest of the saddle herd who was boss.

Now she stood near the fence, and though she didn't look at Jinx, she swished her tail and stamped the hind hoof nearest him. To Sam, it looked like a kind of acceptance, but she wondered what the girls would think.

Could she have guessed which horses had been wild? Sam wondered. Strawberry, Tank, and Amigo all had Quarter horse conformation and muscles built by hard work. Nike was a blood bay and Jeepers-Creepers was an Appaloosa, but both were tall, rangy, and speedy looking. Sweetheart, Gram's aged pinto, was built like a Morgan.

Just like mustangs, they were a mixed bunch.

"You're looking for four wild horses," Brynna said, nudging the girls to guess.

Sam's eyes counted out the mustangs.

Ace, Popcorn, Penny, and Jinx—with coat colors of bay, white, sorrel, and grulla—had once been wild.

She glanced sideways at the two girls.

Behind her glasses, Amelia's hazel eyes were greedy as she studied each horse.

She likes them, Sam thought, and she smiled without meaning to. For the first time, she felt something beyond obligation—like a shared interest in horses— might make her like Amelia.

Amelia's lips parted. But before she ventured a guess, she darted a look at Crystal.

Crystal frowned as she considered her nails and pressed back the cuticle on her index finger.

Seeing that, Amelia kept quiet.

"I guess you'll just have to be surprised," Brynna said. She started walking toward the barn. Sam thought her stepmother was trying to hide her disappointment that the girls refused to guess, until she said, "Let's go see our new baby."

"Aren't you going to tell us?" Crystal asked. As she hurried after Brynna, she demanded of Sam, "Shouldn't we know which ones are wild?"

Was she scared? Sam considered the idea for a minute, but that couldn't be it. The HARP program was voluntary. No one who was afraid of horses would apply.

"I'll make sure you get the horse that's right for you," Brynna said over her shoulder, and Sam knew her stepmother had heard everything.

Though Amelia was clearly eager to see the foal, she stayed in step with Crystal. Sam was already peering through the fence rails at the barn corral when they caught up.

With her legs tucked under her gleaming black body, Tempest slept. Dark Sunshine stood beside her foal, ears pinned back in warning. Her buckskin neck jutted out from tense shoulders, cautioning the newcomers to stay back.

Reading Sunny's threat, Amelia stopped a few feet from the fence and just peered through the rails as Sam had.

Crystal stepped on the lowest rail, swung up her other foot, then climbed up two more rails and rested her arms on the top of the fence.

"The baby's cute. Make her get up," Crystal said.

Was she talking to Brynna?

No one responded except Tempest.

Disturbed by the voice or maybe warned by her mother's circling, Tempest awoke.

"She's just a week old," Brynna explained.

Tempest's head bobbed unsteadily for an instant, but then her small hooves scrabbled against the dirt and propelled her up. Alert brown eyes, wide nostrils, and ears no longer than Sam's little finger took in all there was to learn about the humans at the fence.

Then, without a trace of shakiness, the filly raced to the far side of her mother. Protected by the barricade of Sunny's body, Tempest peeked under her mother's belly.

"Ohh," Amelia sighed.

"I pick her to be my horse," Crystal said.

"Sam and I haven't decided if we'll use Dark Sunshine," Brynna said.

"That's the buckskin's name?" Amelia asked. She covered her lips then, as if she hadn't meant the words to escape.

Amelia knew something about horses, Sam thought. Identifying Sunny's color proved that.

"I want the little scared one," Crystal said, impatiently. "How am I supposed to know her name?"

Sam wanted to growl an answer, but she'd known the girl for less than an hour.

"I'm sorry, Crystal," Sam told her. "Tempest is mine. She's not a HARP horse. Besides, Brynna's got a whole list of things HARP expects you to do by the end of the week, including ride your horse."

That wasn't the real problem. If Amelia had said she'd like to work with Tempest, Sam might have suggested she pet and rub the filly, teaching her to trust humans.

"If you think I can learn to ride a horse after a few days, you're crazy," Crystal said.

"You will." Brynna's voice was meant to comfort Crystal. "But I guess that means you've never ridden?"

"Never even touched one of them," Crystal said proudly.

What was going on? Crystal seemed to be patting herself on the back for duping whoever screened kids for the HARP program.

A cool breeze signaled evening wasn't far off.

Sam stepped out of the barn's lengthening shadow as if she could escape her sudden dread. If Crystal didn't like horses, what was she doing here?

Chapter Six ❧

The aroma of Gram's cooking wafted onto the front porch and welcomed them into the kitchen.

Crystal and Amelia would eat every meal with the family. Both looked uneasy about it, especially when Brynna disappeared upstairs, leaving Sam to introduce them to Gram.

At first, Sam couldn't figure out why the girls regarded Gram with such wariness. She wore a bright lilac apron over her jeans and blouse. Her gray hair was coiled into a smooth bun and her lined face glowed with the confidence that any problem could be cured with a good meal.

Then Sam noticed Crystal and Amelia focusing

on the heavy gunmetal-gray object Gram held in her right hand.

"What is that?" Crystal asked, nodding at the hammer-shaped implement.

Gram laughed. "I call it a tenderizer, though it probably has another name in proper cooking circles." Gram set the utensil aside. "Looks kind of menacing, doesn't it, but it's used for pounding meat so that it's more tender when it's cooked. We're having chicken-fried steak for dinner.

"In fact, once you two have helped Sam put the leaf in the table and washed up, I'll need you, Crystal, to make sure the gravy's not lumpy and Amelia, as soon as the bread's cooled, I'd like you to slice it."

Sam showed Amelia and Crystal how to pull each end of the kitchen table to leave a gap in the middle. Then she retrieved the polished wooden piece—Sam hoped neither girl asked why it was called a leaf—which fit between them, making the table that usually seated four big enough to accommodate six.

Sam pulled a white cloth from a drawer and flapped it over the table. Then she gathered handfuls of silverware and noticed Crystal and Amelia were just standing there, arms crossed, looking out of place.

When Amelia's hand dropped to her pocket to retrieve her cell phone, Sam handed her the silverware.

"Here," she said. "You can set the table with these.

And Crystal," Sam told the dark-haired girl as she took a stack of folded cloth napkins from their drawer, "why don't you put these out?"

Crystal stared at the napkins as if Sam had offered her a porcupine.

Sam tried to understand the girl's reaction. Was it reluctance to help? Or maybe, since Crystal lived alone with her father, they hadn't made a big deal of meals like Gram did.

"They're napkins," Sam said.

"I know what they are, *cowgirl*," Crystal snarled. "I don't live in the backwoods like some people."

Silence filled the kitchen.

It was getting harder to be tolerant of Crystal, but Sam gave it another try.

"I'm sorry—" she began.

"Look, HARP didn't say anything about being a maid." Crystal jerked the napkins from Sam's hand and tossed one at each place setting.

Amelia rubbed her forearms and made a fretting sound just as Brynna came back into the kitchen with Dad.

Brynna introduced Dad and snatched a raw carrot stick from those Gram had arranged on a vegetable platter.

"I heard some discussion of chores," Brynna said. "Since Sam is assisting me in teaching you about horses, you'll help her with chores. Just about anything you're asked to do"—Brynna made eye contact with each girl—"like feeding and watering the animals, helping with the laundry or kitchen work, Sam would do alone if you weren't here.

"Now, I'd like you to wash your hands before you help Grace with the—?" Brynna looked at Gram.

"Gravy and bread," Gram supplied as she mounded black olives in the center of the vegetable plate.

Crystal looked ready to make another protest. Instead, she sighed, "Whatever."

But that implied she was agreeing to the plan, and Sam could tell Crystal was not being agreeable. Brynna and Dad weren't fooled. And neither was Gram.

The minute the girls had come into the kitchen, Gram had told Crystal she'd stand at the stove to whisk gravy instead of trusting her with the bread knife.

Gram had sized up Crystal right away.

After the dinner dishes were washed and dried, Gram and Dad stayed in the kitchen to go over the ranch accounts, while Brynna, Sam, Amelia, and Crystal sat in the quiet living room.

"Leave the television off, please," Brynna said when Crystal paused in front of it.

Sam sat at one end of the couch, nearly squirming in the quiet. If it had been winter, at least they'd have had the crackle of a fire in the fireplace to fill the silence.

Crystal sat in the room's largest armchair, icy-blue

eyes staring at Brynna. Amelia sat on the armchair's ottoman, chewing her already short fingernails.

Brynna sat cross-legged at the opposite end of the couch, stockinged feet pulled up as she flipped through a thick file folder.

Her ease in this awkward situation reminded Sam of how smoothly Brynna dealt with her duties as manager of the Willow Springs Wild Horse Center. Even though she had employees, adopters, a budget, government regulations, and all the controversy swirling around Nevada's wild horses to handle, Brynna loved her job.

Her casual authority said, loud and clear, that a couple of cranky eighth graders weren't going to get her down.

"Here's what's happening this week," Brynna said. "It will deviate a little from what you've been led to expect, but the success of the HARP program depends on making it fit the individuals involved."

"In other words," Crystal said, tossing a lock of black hair back over her shoulder, "now that you've met us, you're changing everything."

"A few things," Brynna said. "But you're not the only factor I'm considering. We've got a new horse."

Sam sat up straighter. They would be using Jinx, then. Great! Despite the gelding's fearsome speed, Sam wanted to ride him.

"During the six days you're here, you'll get to know your horse, learn to groom him," Brynna numbered the first two tasks on her fingers: "Halter, lead, and tie on day three, saddle and bridle, and then on days five and six, we'll have you riding."

"Which horses are we getting?" Amelia asked.

Brynna smiled. "I haven't quite decided, but let me tell you a little about each one."

Sam snuggled back into the couch and listened. Crystal crossed one leg tightly over the other and jiggled her foot. Amelia interlocked her fingers and rocked a little.

"First, you know all these horses are here because they need a second chance, right? They were wild, then captured, then adopted by people who . . ." Brynna's voice trailed off.

"Got sick of them?" Crystal interrupted.

"Not exactly," Brynna said. "They just weren't up to the challenge of a mustang."

Crystal snorted. "Yeah, like we are."

Sam ached to remind Crystal that *she* was a challenge and that's why she was here. But Brynna probably wouldn't like that.

"Popcorn is the white horse. The one with blue eyes like Crystal's," Brynna began. "He's tall for a mustang and he was abused. Not on purpose, but his adopters thought the way to teach him to carry a rider was to 'break' him, to show him who was boss. They thought horses were born to carry riders and the faster he learned how, the sooner he'd be a happy horse."

Amelia drew in a loud breath, then blushed when

all eyes turned to her. "It's, uh," she giggled, "sort of like parents who say 'we're doing this for your own good.'"

"Exactly like that," Brynna agreed.

It must have been the approval in Brynna's tone that made Crystal glare at Amelia. Just the same, Brynna kept talking.

"Anyway, after Popcorn had been shown who was boss one time too many, he became impossible to catch and his adopters returned him to the BLM.

"Penny had a similar experience. She was trained to saddle and then she developed the habit of rearing. . . ."

As Brynna described the horse, Sam noticed the difference in the girls' reactions. Crystal fidgeted in boredom, but Amelia leaned forward, listening as if she could picture each incident.

"They hired a horse trainer, supposedly a professional," Brynna said. "His solution was to jerk the reins tight and pull Penny over backward each time she reared. He would jump clear, of course."

"Did that teach her?" Amelia asked, frowning.

"It hurt her. Badly," Brynna said.

Even Crystal was paying attention now.

"Which one is she?" Crystal asked.

"The little blind sorrel," Brynna said.

"Blind? You're not going to make one of us take her. What can a blind horse do?" Crystal rolled her eyes.

"You might be surprised." Brynna's voice vibrated with anger.

Sam knew her stepmother loved Penny and had little patience with people who thought the mare was useless because she was blind.

Brynna went on more quickly after that, as if her patience was waning.

"And then there's Dark Sunshine, the buckskin with the foal," Brynna said. "She was abused as well—starved, whipped, and used as bait in a trap for other wild horses."

Amelia's pale fingers were interlaced and twitching, but she kept quiet.

"Jinx is the new horse. You saw Wyatt unloading him. He's our mystery mustang, and even though we don't know much about him yet, he carries his history with him in that freeze brand on his neck."

"What's that supposed to mean?" Crystal asked.

Brynna ignored the girl's impatience.

"The brand is made up from the Alpha Angle alphabet." Brynna stopped and her eyes met Sam's. "It's code, sort of, and I'll let you decipher it so you can learn how old he is and where he came from."

"He's kind of a weird color," Amelia ventured. "What is it?"

"Grulla," Sam answered.

"A grew-ya?" Amelia asked quietly.

"In Spanish," Brynna began, "it means crane—"

"Like machinery or one of those gawky birds?" Crystal asked.

"The bird," Brynna said, keeping her voice level. "Probably the blue-gray ones."

"They're a symbol of peace, too," Sam said. She wasn't sure why she put that in, except there was something in the neglected horse that looked like it needed a bit of peace.

"We have another mustang on the ranch, too," Brynna said. "Sam's horse Ace. But he's not part of the HARP program."

"Why not?" Crystal asked.

"Because his adoption, here at River Bend Ranch, has worked out like most. He's happy to be here and we're happy to have him."

"I bet he'd run away if he had the chance," Crystal sneered.

"Actually, he's had a few chances," Sam admitted. "When we first got together, I fell off a lot."

Sam didn't add that Ace had even been back to the valley of wild horses, where he'd once lived, and still returned home with her. She was the only one in the world who knew.

"As sort of a preview of what will be coming, we'll use Sam as a guinea pig," Brynna said.

"We will?" Sam asked.

It wasn't like she couldn't do the things Brynna had described. She'd bet she could groom, halter, saddle, and bridle Ace even if she was blindfolded. But a warning that she'd be "onstage" would have been nice.

"Surprise," Crystal chirped.

Brynna ignored Crystal, but her eyes met Sam's and urged her to cooperate.

"I think it will be a good experience for all of us to see how you do with an unfamiliar horse," Brynna said. "Dallas is working with Jinx right now, making sure he's not an outlaw."

"Oh good, at least we'll know if he's trained to saddle." Sam laughed, but her nerves became jittery.

She wasn't like Jake, who could stick his boot toe in the stirrup and know what to expect by the time his other leg had cleared the horse's back and he'd settled into the saddle. She just wasn't that confident.

"If you don't want to do it—" Crystal began.

At first, Sam was amazed at Crystal's understanding, but then she caught the girl's sly grin. Crystal wasn't sympathizing; she wanted Sam and Brynna to fight.

"I *do* want to do it," Sam said.

"Sure you do," Amelia teased, seconding Crystal's taunt.

There were only two of them, but Amelia and Crystal reminded Sam of the jeering circles of kids that tightened around fights at school, egging on the combatants.

Some people enjoyed conflict, as long as they didn't get hurt.

Sam stood.

"If you don't need me," she told Brynna, "I'll go ask Dallas what he thinks about Jinx."

"I'm just going to go over a few more details, Sam. We'll join you soon," Brynna said.

"Isn't that cheating?" Crystal asked.

"Isn't what cheating?" Brynna looked puzzled.

"If Sam's, like, our role model, and we're going to have to face these horses without knowing anything about them, how come she gets to go ask Dallas— whoever he is—about the grew-ya?"

"I've just told you all you need to know about the horses," Brynna reasoned.

Sam wished Brynna would make Crystal behave. She also wished Brynna would change her mind about exiling her to the bunkhouse with these two. In real life, she'd never choose to spend the night with them.

Most of all, Sam hoped Dallas would declare Jinx too wild to ride or sweet as a lamb, because she didn't want these girls to see her fail.

Chapter Seven ❧

Blaze walked so close to Sam's leg, he kept bumping into her.

"Careful, boy!" Sam gasped as she tripped. The dog scuttled backward, getting clear before she fell on him.

Sam almost told Blaze to sit and stay. He'd do it, and only bark if something out of the ordinary happened. But she didn't have the heart to leave the border collie behind.

Blaze cocked one ear, waiting for her order. His tongue hung from his panting mouth and his eyes looked anxious.

"Things are a little weird today, aren't they, Blaze?"

Sam ruffled the fur on both sides of his neck, then looked at the cowboys' bunkhouse where Blaze spent half his time.

In the summer, the River Bend cowboys usually left their bunkhouse door ajar. Sometimes they'd sit on the step while Dallas played the guitar or, if his hands were sore with arthritis, they'd listen as he played the harmonica. Often the door stood open so that the evening breeze cooled them as they played cards or watched television.

Tonight the door was closed. Light came through the windows, but Pepper and Tank were shy and Dallas was in the round pen, testing Jinx. Sam had a feeling the cowboys were as unsettled as Blaze by the arrival of Crystal and Amelia.

Sam heard the jingle of spurs and slap of leather before the voice.

"I know this horse," Dallas said as he emerged from the round pen, leading Jinx.

Before his words sunk in, Sam saw Dallas as the HARP girls would. He looked exactly as a ranch foreman should.

Gray-haired and bowlegged, Dallas had the walk of a lifelong cowboy. He rode horses, whittled bits of wood into figures, and told details about local life in a way that made them sound like legends.

Dallas had been on the ranch since Sam was born. Even though he didn't share Sam's attachment to mustangs, most of the time he tolerated her feelings with good humor.

Right now, he coaxed Jinx to stand still for a pat.

The gelding was sweated up and nervous. He rolled his brown eyes until the whites showed, but Dallas pretended nothing was wrong as he petted the grulla's neck.

"You know him?" Sam asked.

"Sure," Dallas nodded. "Can't be another grulla with a broken heart brand on his shoulder. Brynna told me not to brush him out. She wants you to do it tomorrow in front of the girls." Dallas shook his head and gave a disapproving frown, then added, "He used to be called Jinx."

"He still is," Sam said. Though it was hard to believe Dad hadn't told Dallas the gelding's name, she guessed that was an example of the differences between them. Dad and Dallas saw horses as just another part of doing ranch business.

"The Potters got him years ago. I see he's got a freeze brand, but I never knew he was a mustang. He musta been a yearling, or a little older when I first saw him," Dallas mused.

The Potters. Sam remembered the name from before her accident. She thought they'd had a child her age, but she couldn't remember if it was a boy or girl.

"Didn't they move away?" Sam hazarded a guess.

She almost remembered a conversation with Jake in which he'd tried to fill in some of what had happened while she was in San Francisco.

"Yep. They up and sold the Happy Heart Ranch and became millionaires."

The Happy Heart Ranch. Sam looked at the broken heart scar on the gelding's shoulder. That name explained the brand, but then she thought of a big billboard she'd seen every day from the school bus window.

"Did that have anything to do with the housing tract near Darton? Happy Heart Homes?" Sam asked, but Dallas was already nodding. "I always thought it was an embarrassing name," Sam admitted. "But it used to be a ranch?"

"'Course." Dallas nodded a few times, as if gathering momentum for a story. "Old man Potter was always a saving sorta guy."

"'Saving'? Do you mean he was stingy?" Sam asked.

"Stingy would be a compliment. Why, there was men refused to throw down their bedrolls near him on cattle drives. Afraid Potter'd steal the gold outta their teeth while they were sleeping."

Sam laughed. "And Jinx was a cow pony on the Potter ranch?"

Dallas nodded. "Potter said he shoulda noticed the horse was a jinx right off, the way that colt acted. See, he had a habit of playing chicken with the fence."

Sam tried to picture that. "You mean he charged the fence and then—"

"—stopped just short of ramming into it," Dallas confirmed.

"That doesn't sound safe," Sam said. Wooden fences could shatter into giant splinters. "What do you suppose made him do that?"

"At first, he was probably tryin' to get up his courage to jump," Dallas said. "And then, I expect it just got to be sort of a game.

"In fact, I remember drivin' by Potter's spread and seein' that pretty blue colt tryin' it. Made me think he'd make a good ropin' horse. You know how they skid to a stop in a cloud of dust and set back on their heels against the rope?"

Sam nodded, considering Jinx's muscular quarters.

"Did they use him as a cow pony?" she asked.

"After a while. First they kept him in a pen, hoping the swelling in his stifles would go down. He tried to charge the fences in the ranch yard, too, and some hand of Potter's got the puny-brained idea to stand on the other side of the fence and snap a bull-whip in the colt's face every time he did it."

Sam sighed. "So did that work?"

"Sure," Dallas said. "But I pity the fool that takes out a whip around this horse."

"Do you think he remembers?" Sam asked.

"I'd say that's the sort of thing a horse don't forget. Hard to tell, though. Never heard stories about his breakin', so he must not have taken the saddle and bridle too hard."

"Why did they name him Jinx? Do you remember?" Sam asked.

"Well, I don't know what he was called when he was first added to Potter's string of saddle horses, but I know one day soon after, Potter was mountin' up in the rain, and he slipped. He'd just been raising his boot toward the stirrup and his other boot slithered through the mud."

Sam shrugged a little. That was nothing that should give the horse the designation Jinx.

"Potter tried to break his fall by stickin' out his arm, and darned if he didn't fracture his wrist, instead." Dallas shrugged. "Claimed he never could rope after that."

Sam sighed. Even in modern times, a rider with a rope could solve problems a rancher in a truck couldn't. He could pull a cow from a river, and move rocks or branches that had fallen in a storm and blocked a road.

"And that was just the beginning," Dallas said. "I can't remember all of it, but you know how things seem monstrous important once folks start looking for them."

"They seem to find what they're looking for," Sam said, nodding. She couldn't help remembering when Rachel Slocum tried to make people at school think Sam had brain damage from her riding accident. Other students had watched her so intently, *Sam* had started wondering about herself.

She wished there was a way to tell Jinx she understood.

"And then there was this pack of feral dogs harassing Potter's stock. Those dogs had already downed a calf when they got to the pasture where Jinx lived. They were about to set after the horses, but when the leader of the pack—a big black Chow with a purple tongue, as I heard it—jumped up, he hit a fence rail and flat knocked himself unconscious."

"But wouldn't that be good luck instead of bad?" Sam asked.

"Depends on your point of view," Dallas said. He seesawed his hand from side to side, and Jinx shied to the end of his reins.

Sam clucked her tongue quietly and walked toward Jinx with her palm held flat. The gelding raised his head, and though he didn't sniff for a familiar scent, he kept his side glance fixed on her.

"I guess the last straw was that Potter was riding Jinx on the day he got word a handful of his heifers had some bovine fever, and the entire herd would have to be quarantined. That meant missing the best prices for his beef, and I guess he was looking for someone or something"—Dallas nodded toward Jinx—"to blame for his misfortune."

"It didn't help cure his superstitions, when, just after he sold off Jinx, the offer came to sell his property for a subdivision with six houses per acre."

Dallas shook his head at such claustrophobic conditions, then looked toward Darton and the remains of the Happy Heart Ranch. "Last I heard, the Potters moved to Hilo, Hawaii or some such place. I guess they're livin' in fine style."

"Wow," Sam said. Though she wouldn't trade River Bend Ranch for a tropical paradise, she must have sounded envious, because Dallas' stare was a reprimand.

"Too damp for my tastes," Dallas declared.

Just then, Jinx dusted his chocolate-colored lips over Sam's extended palm.

"Good boy," she said.

Jinx jerked back as if they'd never had their eye-to-eye moment on the range.

"I think it's cool you remember so much about him," Sam said. "But, why do you? I mean, is it his color?"

"Grullas aren't all that common," Dallas agreed, "though hard-luck broncs are." He gave the gelding a resounding pat on the shoulder. The horse seemed to like it, shifting his weight toward Dallas. "But it wasn't those things that I've been thinkin' about. What I remember best about this horse is his speed. That's why I figured him for some kind of Quarter Horse or Thoroughbred cross. He was the fastest horse I'd ever seen."

"That's what I keep hearing," Brynna said as she approached, just ahead of the HARP girls.

Sam drew a deep breath. She'd been so caught up in Dallas' recollections of Jinx, she'd forgotten her workday wasn't over.

Tonight she had to chaperone Crystal and Amelia. Of all the duties Brynna had assigned her, this made her the most uneasy.

She'd learned a lot about horses from her family, Jake, books, and experience. So she felt okay about being sort of a teacher's aide on riding and horse care.

But if you didn't count slumber parties, she'd had no experience sharing a bedroom with other girls.

Still, Brynna thought everything would work out and she'd had calm answers for each of Sam's questions.

What if they put something gross in her bed? Sam had asked just last night, on the eve of the girls' arrival.

Brynna had suggested she check her sheets before she slipped between them.

What if they waited until she was asleep and then

snuck out? Brynna had asked where she thought the girls would go. Surrounded by open range, with only cattle and wildlife as near neighbors, a city girl would probably want to stay put.

What if—?

Sam's mind was spinning so fast with last night's questions, that Brynna's approach, now, surprised her.

"Watch each step as Dallas unsaddles Jinx," Brynna told the girls. "You'll be doing it soon."

As Amelia and Crystal moved closer to watch, Brynna put her arm around Sam's shoulders.

"We'll see how it goes the first night," Brynna whispered, as if she'd read Sam's mind. "If you need anything, just run over to the house. Knowing your father, his feet will be on the bedroom floor before you get the screen door open."

Sam laughed and took a good look at Amelia and Crystal. Both girls seemed to have settled down. Crystal wasn't looking all around as if planning an escape, and Amelia's hands hung relaxed at her sides.

They watched Dallas work with Jinx as if they were memorizing his motions.

"I guess it's just because I haven't done anything like this before," Sam said.

"And Crystal didn't get off to a smooth start with either of us," Brynna conceded. "So don't be afraid to back out of this part of the job."

Sam didn't like the sound of that. She wasn't a quitter.

"Sam? Really. There's a simple solution. Tomorrow night we'll trade places. You'll sleep in the house and I'll take the bunkhouse if it turns out that you can't handle it."

Chapter Eight ✑

Knee-high sunflowers bordered the path leading up to the new bunkhouse. Gram had planted the flowers among the boulders that edged the path. Sam thought they looked cute and cheerful, but neither Amelia nor Crystal noticed.

The bunkhouse smelled of fresh-sawed pine. Wood stain had been brushed on to give the boards a golden glow. Compared to the cowboys' bunkhouse, it looked like a vacation spot, no matter what Crystal said.

"Good night, Blaze," Sam said as they reached the bunkhouse door, but the dog didn't return to the ranch house.

Instead, he flopped down with a grunt across the

sunflower-lined path. No one would leave without Blaze noticing.

Sam opened the door and flicked on the light as they went inside.

Instantly, Crystal crowded past.

"I'm first in the bathroom," she said.

"Go ahead," Amelia was saying as the door slammed shut.

There's a shock, Sam thought, sarcastically, but she didn't say it.

Right away, Amelia settled in a corner. Sitting cross-legged on one of the two colorful floor pillows Brynna had bought, She pulled out her cell phone and began tapping the keypad.

"What are you playing?" Sam asked.

"It's new," Amelia said without looking up. "I doubt you'd know it."

Neither girl was very polite, Sam thought. Though manners weren't something she thought about much, it was easy to notice when they were missing.

She saw that Crystal and Amelia had claimed two lower bunks of the three bunk beds by leaving their suitcases on them.

Sam blew her cheeks full of air, then let it out. She'd wanted to sleep in an upper bunk, just for fun, but if Amelia and Crystal were going to be able to swing their feet to the floor, she guessed she should be, too.

Sam glanced at Amelia in time to see the younger girl's shoulders hunch as if she were trying to hide.

That would be impossible. Though the bunkhouse was big, with lots of windows to let in sunlight, it was mostly open space. The three beds were clustered at this end, closets ran along one wall, and a long couch covered with golden-brown corduroy sat against the other. The bathroom took up the opposite end of the bunkhouse, but it wasn't luxurious. It had a shower, mirror, and row of cubbies for toiletries.

"No television, no CD player, not even a radio." Amelia didn't look up as she lamented her sad situation. "Crystal noticed that when we first put our stuff in here."

"It's only for a few days," Sam reminded her.

"You've got that stuff in the house," Amelia pointed out.

"Yeah," Sam agreed. She didn't know what to say, or if she should feel guilty.

Amelia closed her phone with a click, slipped it under the big orange pillow, then crossed the bunkhouse to unzip the duffel bag on her bed. She took out pajamas and a makeup kit.

"Lights out at ten, right?" Amelia said.

Her matter-of-fact tone made Sam guess Amelia had been in some sort of rule-crammed facility before the HARP program.

"Yeah," Sam said again.

She walked around, pulling the curtains closed on

each of the windows, then glanced at her watch. It was only nine thirty! She couldn't stand the idea of being in here with two hostile strangers for another half hour.

"I want to go check on Tempest and Dark Sunshine," she told Amelia.

Excitement brought a flush to the girl's pale face and Sam knew she'd made the right move.

She hurried. If she gave Amelia time to think, she'd whine that Crystal should come along. Crystal *should*, but Sam would bet her summer's paycheck the dark-haired girl would refuse.

"Crystal," Sam yelled at the closed bathroom door. "We're going down to the barn and check on the new foal. Do you want to come?"

A few seconds of silence passed before Crystal asked, "Why?"

What kind of question was that? Sam wondered. Automatically she glanced at Amelia, who shrugged. Sam hid her smile. Something in Amelia's reaction made them a team, at least for a moment.

"For fun," Sam called back.

"Yeah, well, I've had about all the *fun* I can stand today. I'm not going down to sniff horse manure." Crystal paused for a reaction. When it didn't come, she added, "Amelia, are you leaving me here alone?"

You creep, Sam thought.

She didn't turn around to look at Amelia.

"Come with us, Crystal," Amelia begged.

"No way," Crystal shouted back.

"Please?" Amelia whined.

Sam couldn't believe Amelia thought that would convince the other girl.

It didn't. They heard running water, and humming, but no answer from Crystal. Crystal was banking on Amelia's weakness.

When Sam turned, Amelia's hands were linked together. Her fingers clutched each other as if she were wringing water from a sponge.

"Crystal will be fine here. We'll only be across the yard," Sam told Amelia.

"Well . . ."

"Besides, I have to go see Tempest."

"The filly," Amelia said.

"Yeah, she's sort of my baby," Sam confessed. "I was here alone, in a lightning storm with no power, on the night she was born."

"No," Amelia gasped, and her hunched shoulders straightened.

Now. Sam headed for the door. Amelia might forget about being Crystal's follower if the pull of the horses was stronger.

Sam opened the door, stepped over Blaze, and remained still for a minute. Heat radiated from the boulders edging the path, even though it was full dark. Crickets chirped in the grass and moonlight painted the ranch yard in shades of gray and white.

"Stay, boy," Sam said when the border collie

scrambled to his feet.

Recognizing an order, he sat obediently.

"Are you putting him on guard so Crystal doesn't escape?" Amelia asked, standing in the doorway.

That was exactly what she was doing, so Sam didn't deny it. Instead, she told a different truth.

"Actually, he makes Dark Sunshine kind of nervous," Sam said, and then she just started walking.

The bunkhouse door closed and the next sound she heard was Amelia's footsteps hurrying to catch up.

Sam turned on the barn's overhead lights. Beside her, Amelia took a deep breath of hay and horses. Sam glanced over, smiling, but Amelia was—touching her temples? Sam looked away. She'd turned so quickly, she wasn't sure if Amelia was rubbing away a headache or wiping away tears.

Sam didn't ask.

When she'd first moved back to River Bend, she'd noticed how much Westerners respected privacy.

Gram had joked that the habit was rooted in the old days, when people came out West fleeing scandal. Jake thought it was from the old days, too, but he said toting a gun made people more polite. Dad and Brynna said respect for privacy was bred by space. When miles of range, desert, or mountains separated you from neighbors, minding your own business came naturally.

Whatever had caused it, Sam decided to respect Amelia's privacy. Amelia would talk when she was ready. Until then, maybe the horses could help her.

Amelia stood sideways to the stall, letting Dark Sunshine approach slowly. Yes, Sam thought, this girl had definitely been around horses before.

"She's beautiful, isn't she?" Amelia sighed. "Look at her pretty butterscotch coat. You take good care of her."

Sam supposed Amelia could be kissing up like she did with Crystal, but she didn't think so.

"Sunny's had a tough time," Sam explained. "I've done what I can, but she still doesn't trust people."

"That's smart, don't you think?" Amelia asked, hesitantly.

"No one here will harm her," Sam insisted.

"How can she believe that? I think it's way intelligent that's she's learned not to do what got her hurt."

Dark Sunshine sniffed at her between the boards and Amelia shivered with pleasure.

"I guess so," Sam agreed.

Amelia's words made sense, but Sam had the feeling the younger girl was talking about herself, as well as the mare.

"You like horses, don't you?" Sam asked.

For the first time, Amelia's expression had real force. "If I didn't, why would I be here?"

"Good point," Sam said, knowing better than to bring up Crystal.

"I took English riding lessons when I was ten,"

Amelia snapped. "They were a present from my grandparents, but the first time I got in trouble, my dad made me quit."

"I hate that," Sam sympathized.

"Hate what?" Amelia demanded.

"If I really get in trouble—and it's happened, believe me—I get grounded from riding Ace," she said. "I know it's not as bad, but—"

"No, it isn't. My dad took everything away from me. My music, my books, and he even ripped my posters off the walls. I live in a bare room with just my bed and chest of drawers.

"I could have taken that, but when I couldn't go to lessons, that was the end of riding for me. Just when my teacher said I was a *natural*." Amelia ended in a whisper.

Blaze yipped and Sam was pretty sure Crystal had decided to leave the bunkhouse, but Amelia didn't notice.

"Here's the stupid thing: I was actually honest with him."

"Your dad?"

"Yeah, I told him my friends at the stable were the ones helping me stay out of trouble. My friends in the neighborhood kept after me to steal stuff with them—"

"That's real nice," Crystal's sarcastic voice came from the dark outside the barn. Then she appeared in the doorway. "Ratting out your friends, huh?"

Amelia giggled. Her eyes changed, taking on a sly

look as she said, "Not really. I was just saying that."

The switch happened so quickly, Sam couldn't guess which was the real Amelia.

Crystal joined Amelia's laughter. Together, the girls' merriment was—Sam stopped. The word that popped into her head was something Gram would say. But it was the only one that fit. Together, Amelia and Crystal sounded *vulgar*.

"What's that?" Crystal's hands flew up to cover her hair before Sam noticed the rustling overhead.

"Pigeons," Sam said. "They live up there."

"Not bats? Are you sure?" Crystal backed toward the doorway. "Let's get out of here."

"Okay," Amelia said. Without a word or glance, she turned to follow Crystal back to the bunkhouse.

The blue-green numbers on Sam's watch glowed in the still-dark bunkhouse. Five thirty. In the morning.

Sam yawned. She'd stayed awake until midnight, even though the girls had sounded like they were asleep.

She was supposed to get up and have a meeting with Brynna. Five thirty was insanely early to get out of bed on a summer morning.

Sam buried her face in her pillow. They didn't need a meeting. But the rooster crowed from the hen-house, refusing to let her doze.

Mentally grumbling, Sam slipped out of bed.

"What?" Amelia sat straight up in her bunk. Her hazel eyes looked wide without glasses to hide them.

"You scared me half to death," Sam hissed at her. "Go back to sleep. You have another hour."

Amelia stared, then lowered her head to her pillow.

Heart still pounding, Sam picked up her boots and carried them as she tiptoed from the bunkhouse.

Sunflowers nudged Sam's arm as she sat on one of the boulders to pull on her boots. A starling's creaky call mixed with the sounds of fretting hens, but Blaze wasn't on guard. After the girls were settled last night, he must have trotted off to join the cowboys.

Sam's knees and shoulder joints felt like they were filled with sand. They cracked and popped, though she couldn't remember doing anything especially strenuous yesterday. Maybe sleeping in a strange bed was enough.

Get used to it, she told herself.

Then, as she walked across the ranch yard, she noticed the horses in the ten-acre pasture seemed to have divided into two herds. Most were at the far end, grazing, but Popcorn and Ace watched her from the fence line closest to Jinx.

Ace's nicker floated through the morning. When she clucked a greeting back, he stamped a front hoof, but stayed where he was.

By the time Sam reached the kitchen, she was wide awake and bursting with the news that the three mustangs might have banded together.

"Good morning, dear," Gram said. She held her hands, sticky with bits of bread dough, clear of Sam as she kissed her cheek.

"Mornin'," Dad said as he came into the kitchen. "Got you a head start on wakin' up." He nodded toward the cup of hot chocolate waiting on the kitchen table.

Sam blew curls of steam from the surface of her hot chocolate, waiting for it to cool while Dad poured coffee for himself and Brynna.

"I don't know why I'm so sleepy," Brynna said as she padded into the kitchen in jeans and a long-sleeved white shirt. She was barefooted and still braiding her hair.

Sam laughed. Brynna got up early every morning, but she never seemed to get used to it. Sam watched her stepmother take an experimental sip of coffee, then sigh.

"So, how did it go last night?" Brynna asked.

"Not bad." Sam explained how Crystal kept acting bossy and Amelia kept giving in.

"It's really only the first day," Brynna said.

"Oh, but I found out something cool." Sam took a quick swallow of her hot chocolate. "Amelia took riding lessons about a year ago."

"Great," Brynna agreed. "That fits perfectly with what I've been thinking. . . ."

"Is that why you were tossing your covers off and

thrashing around all night?" Dad joked.

"Afraid so," Brynna conceded. "And I've about decided I want Crystal to ride Popcorn."

"I thought you wanted the grulla to teach her a lesson," Dad said.

"That was before I knew she was afraid of animals," Brynna said.

"Even the pigeons in the barn rafters," Sam added.

"I didn't think usin' a horse to bring her down a peg was a good idea to begin with," Dad said.

"You were probably right," Brynna agreed. "But we won't know for sure until Sam's finished riding him today."

Dad rubbed his fingertips over his brow. It was a gesture Sam usually saw him make at the end of a long day, not first thing in the morning.

He was afraid she couldn't ride Jinx.

"Dallas said Jinx was fine," Sam told him.

"He was fine for *Dallas*," Dad pointed out.

"I won't let her do anything risky," Brynna promised.

"It's your call," Dad said.

Sam felt a little sorry for Brynna. Dad had a way of making you take responsibility that sounded downright scary. "I'm going out brush-poppin' with Ross and Pepper, but I don't want to come home to any surprises."

Brush-poppin' meant riding through ravines

clogged with sagebrush, searching out cattle that might have hidden during the recent roundup.

Sam felt a little envious, but Dallas' story about Jinx had made her eager to lavish attention on the misunderstood horse.

As she walked away from the ranch house, Sam imagined how beautiful the curried and cared-for Jinx would look.

The sun had risen and it was almost too warm when she stepped inside the new bunkhouse.

"My hair's going to turn orange," Crystal accused, grabbing Sam's arm to drag her into the bathroom.

Crystal pointed at the floor of the shower.

"Do you mean those streaks?" Sam said. "There's iron in the water. Just wipe it out."

"I was worried about my hair, not your shower," Crystal bawled, but as soon as she paused for a breath, Amelia cut in with a second complaint.

"Crystal's not wearing boots, so I'm not going to, either."

"You have to wear boots. Both of you. Today it might not matter, but it will when we mount up. You might as well get used to them."

Sam hadn't meant to sound so bossy, but taking back her words would be a mistake. A shoe without a heel could slip through the stirrup. If the rider fell and the horse kept moving, she could be dragged.

As Sam made up her bunk, she heard Crystal mutter, "Who died and made her queen?"

Go ahead and hate me, Sam thought as she opened the curtains on each window.

Ignoring their unmade beds, the girls stood together at the bathroom mirror. Amelia seemed to be mimicking Crystal's way of applying eye makeup.

"I'll meet you up at the kitchen for breakfast," Sam said.

She sighed as she left the bunkhouse, but it wasn't the sound of her own breath that stopped her three steps down the path.

The whirring noise drew her eyes to the flat-topped boulder she'd sat on just an hour ago.

Nightmares were like this.

You looked.

You saw.

Your cry was strangled to silence by fear.

Chapter Nine ❧

$\mathcal{T}$he snake lay across the boulder like a foot-long mosaic of beige and brown. His forked tongue flicked. The bumps on his tapered tail looked like rows of corn on the cob as they twitched from side to side.

Do rattlesnakes have to be coiled to strike? Can they bite through leather boots? How about jeans? Will it come after me if I back away?

The rattlesnake's seeking head raised off the rock. Its intent eyes glinted.

Sam couldn't remember what to do.

It's more afraid of you than you are of it.

She'd heard that about all kinds of wildlife. She hoped it was true of rattlesnakes.

Sam scuffed her boot on the dirt, trying to frighten

the snake. Like magic, it wove itself into a coil and its rattles beat louder.

Sam took a step backward. The snake didn't seem to notice. She took another silent step away, and another, until her back was pressed against the bunk-house door.

It couldn't reach her from here. Then, even though she was watching, the snake disappeared. She couldn't say which side of the boulder it had flowed down. There was movement and it was gone.

Sam's breath rushed out and she rapped on the closed bunkhouse door. She didn't feel like turning her back on the path. It hadn't been a very big snake. What if its mother were nearby?

The door jerked inward and Sam staggered back a step, laughing in relief.

"What?" Crystal snapped.

Sam covered her mouth against the inappropriate laughter bubbling up in her. She pointed toward the path, and Amelia and Crystal looked.

"A rattlesnake was right there."

"Oh, sure." Crystal's surliness hadn't cured itself overnight.

"I don't care if you believe me. I need to tell my Dad." Sam started toward the ranch house. "And if I were you, I'd stay in the middle of the path."

Dubious but unsure, the girls looked around them.

To Sam, their ankles looked vulnerable above their sneakers.

"And you're idiots if you don't put on boots!"

Sam broke into a jog, suddenly desperate to tell Dad before he left the ranch.

"You can't talk to us like that!" Crystal shouted after her, but Sam kept running.

Brush-poppin' was put off for a few hours.

Wearing thick leather gloves, Dad and the cowboys searched out openings around every exterior door of the house and both bunkhouses and blocked them. They cut down brush that bordered paths, so that snakes wouldn't rest in their shade during the heat of the day.

After a nervous breakfast, Sam sat on the front porch, listening as Brynna gave Amelia and Crystal an impromptu lecture on rattlesnakes. Dad's voice carried as he and the cowboys worked around the barn.

"If the gap's big enough to stick a pencil through, a snake can slip in," he was explaining.

Sam rubbed the gooseflesh from her arms.

"Most of the time we'll be working in the corrals, but when we're not, stay on the paths," Brynna cautioned the girls. "Don't put your hands or feet where you can't see. If you're working with a horse and it snorts, shies, or backs away from what seems to be nothing, pay attention. And for heaven's sake, if you see a snake, don't try to move, touch, or kill it. Go around it. At least six feet around it."

"But they're going to kill them, right?" Amelia's face was paler than before as she gestured toward the cowboys.

"No," Brynna said. "At least, I don't think so."

Sam would bet this was a subject Brynna and Dad might disagree over. Because she was a biologist, Brynna would focus on the balance of nature. But Dad . . .

Clearly Brynna and Dad hadn't yet discussed this topic during their short marriage.

"No?" Crystal said. "If you're not going to kill them, why have this whole snake hunt?"

"To keep us safe," Sam said. "So we don't come upon one accidentally."

Sam kept her voice level, but she couldn't stop thinking that she'd actually sat on that boulder this morning.

The snake had done the same thing she had, picking out a warm place on a cool morning.

"I'm trying to remember everything I know about rattlesnakes, but I'm a little rusty," Brynna said. "I know most snakes around here are harmless. We've got gopher snakes, garter snakes, and king snakes in the mountains, but rattlesnakes are pretty distinctive. Their heads are more triangular and their tails are rounded at the tip—not like our other snakes, which have long, pointy tails."

"Won't your dog chase them away?" Amelia asked.

Brynna glanced toward the house. Blaze stood on the other side of the screen door, panting. He wagged his tail, eager to come out, but Brynna shook her head.

"Snakes are more dangerous to Blaze than to you. Dogs bark until they've got the snake good and worried, then they stick their noses down where they can be bitten.

"Coiling and rattling are defensive behaviors. Rattlesnakes don't have very good eyesight, but if you're too big to be a tasty mouse, they're scared. They're telling you to go away and sometimes they'll even bite."

"What makes you think they're scared, not mean?" Crystal asked.

"Sometimes they don't even inject venom," Brynna said. "You can't count on that, of course, but once in a while they give what's called a dry bite."

Sam had never heard of a dry bite, but she'd seen those fangs in action on a nature show. Poison or no poison, a snake's bite would hurt.

"Lecture over," Brynna said. She stood and slapped her palms on her jeans. "Sam, while I get the brushes and combs for grooming, why don't you walk over and let Jinx know we're coming."

Brynna took off toward the barn. Sam found herself a few steps ahead of Amelia and Crystal as they walked toward the metal pen, but she could hear them talking.

"I don't think there was any snake," Crystal said. "They're doing this to keep us from sneaking out."

"I don't know," Amelia answered. "Sam said—"

"Of course she did. Do you think she wants to be up all night listening for us?"

"No, but—"

"Besides, even if there *was* one, I wouldn't be afraid of it," Crystal bragged. "Think of the stories you could tell if you got one of those dry bites."

"But it would hurt," Amelia protested.

"I bet it would be just like getting a slap," Crystal said. "And I'm not afraid of a little pain."

Crystal's showing off could ruin everything. If she was bitten, the HARP program might hold her injury against everyone at River Bend Ranch.

"Hey Amelia," Sam said over her shoulder. "Could you run back to the kitchen and get a carrot for Jinx?"

Amelia's arms crossed at her waist. "Why don't you do it?"

"Just go ask my grandmother for one," Sam insisted.

"Go ahead." Crystal gave Amelia's shoulder a push.

Looking scared and embarrassed, Amelia went.

"What?" Crystal said to Sam. Her feet were set apart and her hands perched on her hips. "You obviously wanted to get me alone to yell at me."

Crystal focused her pale eyes on Sam.

"There *was* a rattlesnake," Sam insisted. "It's no trick to keep you here."

"Whatever," Crystal said, rolling her eyes.

"Why did you even sign up for HARP?" Sam asked the question that had been brewing in her mind since she'd met the girl. "You don't want to be here. You don't even like animals."

"That's driving you crazy, isn't it?" Crystal said in a low voice. "Well, I have my own reason for being here, and there's nothing you can do about it."

An hour of brushing and currying transformed Jinx. His roached mane looked cocky rather than disreputable, and his glossy tail flowed like black water. His smoky silver-blue coat shone in the June sun. His ears were tipped and edged with dark-chocolate brown, and so were his face and shoulders.

The screen door slammed. Though Gram had been watching from the window, now she came out to the hitching rail and applauded.

"He looks wonderful, Sam," Gram said. "Like sterling silver with a little tarnish in places. Trust you to see his possibilities."

Gram walked closer while Brynna described the horse's markings to Amelia and Crystal.

"That's called leg barring and that's a dorsal stripe," Brynna said, pointing out the shadows on Jinx's hocks and the dark stripe that ran along his spine.

"Like sterling silver," Gram repeated to Jinx as he

nuzzled her hand. "When it hasn't been used for a while." She reached up to rub his poll, then added, "Just polish a little and it shines like new."

Sam stood holding the brush while Gram talked to the horse. Finally, Gram gave him a pet good-bye.

"Just a beauty," Gram was still muttering as she went back inside the house.

As if he'd follow, Jinx pulled back against the halter rope tethering him.

"I guess it's time to saddle up," Brynna said at last.

Saddling was the easy part. Mounting turned out to be impossible.

As Sam poised to swing into the saddle, Jinx began breathing hard. He flicked his ears front, back, and sideways.

"What's wrong, boy?" Sam crooned.

Jinx wasn't acting like a lazy horse. He was scared.

After Sam realized that, Brynna's voice faded to a drone.

Sam was pretty sure Brynna was describing each step she took in coping with the anxious horse, but Sam's mind was locked on Jinx.

"Let's try this slowly," Sam told the gelding.

She took her time gathering her reins, arranging the loose ends over Jinx's right shoulder and placing her left hand at the base of his Mohawk mane. She clucked to him and prepared to bounce up into the stirrup.

Ears pricked toward Sam, Jinx swung his

hindquarters away. He snorted and danced in place.

Five minutes later, when the gelding's flanks and neck had darkened with sweat and she was still trying to mount, Sam asked, "What's scaring you, boy? You are such a good horse," Sam told him. "You're not bucking, kicking, or biting to make your point, but you sure don't want me up there."

Ten minutes later, Jinx was lathered white and Sam's legs shook from her failed attempts to swing into the saddle.

"This isn't normal." Brynna's voice cut through Sam's concentration. "Girls, this happens sometimes, when a horse has been mistreated. You have to read his mind, guess what went wrong in his past and convince him it won't happen again.

"Sam, try taking him into the barn, then put his right side up against the wall and mount him there."

"I can do that," Sam said, nodding. She heard her own breathlessness and she was glad for Brynna's suggestion.

With one side against the barn wall, Jinx couldn't sidestep away from her.

"Once you're up, ride on out and we'll have the gate open to the barn corral. I've already locked Dark Sunshine and Tempest in their stall, so you and Jinx will have the corral to yourselves."

"Good idea," Sam said. Then, with pretend confidence, she led Jinx toward the barn. Whatever bad experiences he'd had must have come from a rider. He'd liked her fine until she'd tried to mount.

As they clopped past the ten-acre pasture, Ace neighed longingly. When Jinx answered, Ace swished his tail and bared his teeth.

"You're still my best boy, Ace," Sam called. She heard Crystal's derisive laughter, but she didn't care.

These horses were more important to her than Crystal.

Despite Ace's glare, Jinx tried to swing toward the pasture. Sam didn't let him.

"Yes, I know you're a herd animal," she said, forcing him to walk beside her. "And I know you want to stay with your new friends, but we're only going across the ranch yard. You'll like the barn. It smells like food and there are horses in there, too."

Jinx allowed himself to be led the rest of the way.

Dark Sunshine's buckskin head bobbed above the side of her stall as Sam and Jinx entered.

Tempest's hooves pattered and jumped. She squealed and shoved her mother, trying to see what was going on.

"That's right," Sam encouraged the mare and foal, "you girls cheer him on. See, Jinx? They know you can do this."

Sam positioned Jinx next to the barn wall, petted him in slow, understanding motions, then exhaled.

"One more time, boy," she said. Then, before Jinx

could move away, Sam touched her boot to the stirrup, and vaulted aboard.

Sam crossed her fingers as she settled in the saddle.

Jinx trembled beneath her, but he didn't bolt or buck. Everything was going to be okay.

Chapter Ten ∾

*J*inx relaxed.

So did Sam. It didn't matter that Brynna and the girls were outside waiting, wondering what was going on inside the barn. If she didn't hear bucking and banging, Brynna wouldn't worry.

Jinx sniffed noses with Dark Sunshine. He stared at a pigeon coasting through the air from one rafter to the next. He whuffled his lips along the barn floor and munched a piece of straw.

"Bad manners," Sam whispered. Dad said a horse that ate with someone in the saddle was showing disrespect for his rider. Sam rubbed the grulla's withers. "But I'll pretend I didn't see, okay?"

Sam's mind buzzed with possible explanations for

the gelding's reluctance to be ridden. She'd like to phone the cowboy who'd sold this horse to Clara and ask some questions. Right now.

Jinx yawned. Sam felt his hindquarters shift as he cocked a rear hoof on its point. Jinx's resistance had tired him out. And, Sam thought as she brushed at her dusty jeans, they could both use some grooming. But now was not the time to relax.

Sam tightened her legs and eased her weight forward. Jinx shook his roached mane, but he understood her signal to leave the barn. Slowly, he did as she asked.

Sam blinked against the sunlight as they emerged from the barn. The gate to the pasture was on her left. Amelia held it open.

"Thanks," Sam said.

Amelia had the good sense not to make any movements or sounds that would startle Jinx as he passed her.

"Just circle the pasture at a walk," Brynna suggested.

So they were going to play horse show, Sam thought. It was a good idea and just what she'd expected. If all went well, Amelia and Crystal would be doing the same by Friday.

Jinx's long, smooth strides carried her around the pasture while Brynna, Crystal, and Amelia watched. Sam felt proud of the horse.

"Try moving into a jog," Brynna called.

As Jinx changed gaits, his muscles stiffened.

Uh-oh. Sam tried not to react. Her tension would telegraph itself to the gelding and make him edgy again.

She rode out Jinx's uneven jog, but she could barely keep her seat.

Jinx gave a longing neigh, as if calling to another horse. Had Dad and the cowboys ridden out? Or had someone else come in? Maybe Jinx was just asking Ace and the other horses for support.

None of those questions or answers mattered.

Jinx had begun mouthing the bit when Brynna—who *must* see what was going on, Sam thought—told her to lope.

When Sam leaned forward, gently urging him into a faster gait, Jinx refused.

"What's wrong, boy?" Sam asked as the horse slowed his choppy trot.

Jinx couldn't answer, and Sam wished Jake were here. Brynna knew a lot and she was good with horses, but the HARP girls were her first priority and she'd be explaining all this to them.

Jake was an instinctive horseman. He'd like helping her figure out what Jinx was thinking.

"Huh, boy?" she clucked her tongue. "What is it?"

In answer, Jinx stopped completely.

He halted so suddenly, Sam caught herself against the grulla's chopped mane. The saddle horn poked her in the stomach.

It hurt, but this was no time to whine.

Quickly, Sam readjusted her position in the saddle and asked the horse to walk.

Legs braced like a four-poster bed, Jinx refused to go on. He didn't buck, kick, or act like he wanted to be the boss. He just stopped.

When nothing else worked, Sam used her reins to pull the gelding's head to one side. The sweat-stiff hair on his neck prickled up as she moved his head farther, a little farther, there! Jinx stepped after his head. Sam used her legs to keep him moving in that direction.

"Good boy," she crowed. "See? Nothing scary about walking around the pasture."

Jinx swished his tail so that it lashed her leg, stinging even through her jeans, but that was his only sign of impatience.

"He's stubborn as a mule. Don't give him to me."

Sam recognized Crystal's voice and wasn't surprised that the girl was too self-centered to see that the grulla was not stubborn, but scared.

When Sam's attention wandered to Crystal, Jinx noticed.

I should have known! The words flashed through Sam's mind as Jinx burst into a gallop.

"Frightening speed." Isn't that how the cowboy had described Jinx's talent to Clara?

Wind tore at Sam's hair as Jinx sped around the pasture. The fact that she *wasn't* frightened astonished her.

Jinx's gait was smooth and natural. For the first time, the horse beneath her felt happy.

Sam and Jinx circled the pasture twice. Colors smeared as if she rode the world's fastest carousel horse. When she felt a faint hesitation in Jinx's gait, she knew it was time to ask him to stop. Would he do it?

Sam sucked in a breath, held it, then barely moved her fingers to make contact with the bit.

Jinx sat back on his heels and slid like a roping horse. With dust still billowing around them, he backed up so fast, his rump slammed into the pasture fence. Then he turned, hooves slamming against the fence as if he'd climb over.

Panic gripped Sam.

But Jinx needed someone to be in control, to tell him what to do. Sam knew it had to be her.

"Jinx, you're okay. You're fine, boy. No one's going to hurt you. Hey Jinxy, you're safe. . . ."

Sam babbled sweet nonsense to the gelding. Finally, he listened. He quieted and stood with hanging head, breath huffing through his lips.

Sweat dripped stinging into Sam's eyes. Her wet bangs stuck to her forehead. She couldn't believe she was still in the saddle.

"And that's how it's done." Brynna's voice wove pride and concern with sarcasm.

Sam glanced at her stepmother. Brynna formed her fingers into an "okay" sign, then gave Sam a smile of disbelief.

In the same glance, Sam took in the fact that Crystal wasn't watching.

That figures, Sam thought, but then she craned her neck to see what the dark-haired girl had noticed.

A black horse nearly hid the male figure.

Suddenly Sam remembered Jinx's neigh. She'd assumed he was calling to the saddle horses, but maybe he'd been greeting Witch.

Witch was Jake's high-spirited Quarter Horse. She stood sideways to the pasture, and Jake sighted over the saddle as if he'd been watching Jinx's one-horse race.

But what was Jake doing here?

"Do you want to dismount and talk about what happened?" Brynna's voice called Sam back to the HARP program.

"No way," she said.

Surprised laughter came from Crystal and Amelia.

"I'm not sure I could ever get back on," Sam explained.

"Maybe Jinx is done for the day," Brynna suggested.

Sam noticed that her stepmother was actually

seeking her opinion. She sighed, wanting to be right in front of the girls and Jake.

"I don't think we should quit now," Sam said.

"A lot of times, a horse begins balking when he's been pushed too hard, beyond his strength," Brynna said.

Sam considered that possibility.

"I can't read Jinx's mind, of course, but I don't think that's what happened to him," Sam said slowly. "Once he started galloping, Jinx was happy. It was before that when he seemed stressed."

"The horse psychic speaks," Crystal joked, but she was the only one laughing.

Sam stared at Brynna.

Brynna stared back.

As they tried to puzzle out the horse's problem, Jinx's dark muzzle swung around. Ears pricked forward, eyes soft, Jinx rubbed his nose against Sam's boot. That wasn't the act of a terrified horse.

"You're the one in the saddle, Sam," Brynna said. "Tell us what you think."

"Okay." Sam's cheeks heated with a blush as she gathered the courage to speak. "What about this. If Jinx has always been a good runner, like Dallas said, and then he got a timid rider, who didn't want him to run—"

"Every time he wanted to stretch his legs and run full out, he'd get punished."

Sam grinned.

The voice was Jake's. If he'd joined in, he must agree with her.

"Hi, Jake," Sam said, and Brynna's voice echoed her greeting.

Amelia cast a quick glance at Jake then turned away, but not Crystal. As Jake lifted a hand in greeting, Crystal tried to catch his attention.

She smoothed her hands over her long hair, twisted it up off her neck, and looked intently at Jake, even when he looked away.

Oh, give me a break, Sam thought. Crystal had just finished seventh grade. Next year Jake would be a senior. And yet, Crystal was looking at Jake like he was—Sam's mind groped for a comparison—chocolate!

Jinx gave an uneasy nicker and Sam rubbed the flat of her palm in circles on his neck.

"Settle down," she murmured to the horse, but she wanted to say the same to Crystal.

What did Crystal think she was doing? She couldn't even see whether or not he was handsome. Jake's face was shaded by the brim of his Stetson.

Maybe that was it. Maybe Crystal was only interested because Jake was a cowboy. She didn't know he was shy. Even when he felt at home with someone, he didn't talk unless he had something to say.

Watching Jake tend to a cinch that didn't need

his attention, Sam made a bet with herself that Jake wouldn't speak to the HARP girls unless he was forced.

"Jake?" Brynna's voice invaded Sam's thoughts. "I'd like you to meet our two students. Amelia, this is our neighbor Jake Ely."

"Hi," Amelia said, ducking her head so that her glasses slid halfway down her nose and her thin hair almost covered her face.

"Nice to meet you," Crystal chirped before Brynna could introduce her. "I'm Crystal. Did we see you at that little town when we were coming in from the airport?"

"Hello," Jake managed, but that was all.

As Crystal's eyes scoured over him, Jake rubbed the back of his neck in discomfort.

No wonder Jake didn't want to be a HARP teacher. He was uneasy and tongue-tied around pushy girls.

Jake's gaze passed the girls and Brynna, soared over the fence, and met Sam's as she sat inside the pasture on Jinx. There was an appeal for rescue in his eyes.

"So, what's up?" she asked him.

"I, uh, need you to . . ." Jake mumbled the rest of the sentence.

"What?" Sam rose in her stirrups as if that could help her hear. She was usually pretty good at understanding Jake, but from this distance, he'd have to speak up.

He made a dismissing motion and tugged at his hat brim.

"Never mind."

Sam sighed. If she got off Jinx now, she wouldn't be able to remount without a fight. Each time that happened, it scarred her relationship with Jinx.

I need you to. . .

To *what*? What had Jake been about to ask her to do? If she let him leave River Bend without explaining, she might miss something interesting.

"Sam?" Brynna said. "I'm going to take the girls back to the house for a cold drink. Can I bring you something? How about you, Jake?"

"Sure," Sam said, silently applauding her stepmother's intuition.

"No thanks," Jake said. He watched Brynna and the girls until they were halfway to the house. Then, leaving Witch ground-tied, he strode toward the pasture gate.

Crystal looked back over her shoulder with a smirk, but she kept walking.

The pasture gate creaked open and Sam rode through.

Though Witch was ground-tied yards away, she flattened her ears and bared her teeth at Jinx.

"We don't want to go over by her, anyway," Sam

told Jinx, and the gelding was happy to follow her directions to walk closer to Jake.

Sam leaned forward so that her face was closer to Jake's and whispered, "What do you need me to do?"

He sighed. "Write a statement for the accident report. Not that it matters. That horse *is* a jinx. I'm going to lose my driver's license."

Chapter Eleven ᖇ

Sam straightened in the saddle. When she tightened her reins and legs, Jinx backed without question—two steps, three, four.

"Good boy." Sam patted Jinx's neck. Then she leaned down to talk to the horse, quietly, but loud enough for Jake to hear. "We had to back up so you could get a good look at this *horseman*, who actually believes you're bringing him bad luck."

Jake's angry expression faded.

"It doesn't put me in a good mood," Jake admitted, "to know the best thing that can happen is I have to pay a ton of money to keep my car insurance, so I can drive."

"What did your mom say about her car?" Sam

asked carefully. Mrs. Ely had been Sam's history teacher during the school year. She made class fun, but Mrs. Ely was tough. She never accepted late homework or excuses.

"Not much, but I have to pay for my insurance now," Jake said. "That means getting a real job this summer."

As the youngest of six brothers on Three Ponies Ranch, Jake did his chores, of course, but he also worked with Sam's dad. Together, they trained and conditioned horses that seemed to have potential, then sold them at a profit. They'd planned to do the same this summer and fall.

"Just train horses with Dad like you planned," Sam suggested.

"Not a dependable income," Jake said. "My dad said I can't count on someone wantin' to buy a horse just 'cause I have one to sell."

"I guess he's right," Sam said. "But I still don't think it was your fault."

"Yeah, well, I don't think so, either." Jake looked down and scuffed his boot toe in the dirt. "But no one's real interested in my opinion."

With his head bent, Jake's black hair, bound with a strip of soft leather at the nape of his neck, fell neatly against his ironed shirt collar. His shoulders might be as broad as Dad's, but right now, Jake looked like a disappointed kid.

"I am," she told him. Then, when he didn't look

up, she added, "I want your opinion, but you have to bite your tongue and not give it to me until I finish asking."

"Yeah?"

Only someone who knew him well would recognize the raised corner of Jake's mouth as the beginning of a smile.

"I want to take Jinx to War Drum Flats and run him. He was fast yesterday, but I want to try him with a rider this time. Me. Now," she rushed on, when Jake took a breath, "because Jinx is tired, and easier to handle."

Jinx blew through his lips as if to prove her point.

"Crystal, Amelia, and Brynna could follow in the truck," Sam said. Then, half because it was true and half to tease Jake, she added, "Crystal might think it was exciting. Although, you're the only thing that's really piqued Crystal's interest since she —"

"Don't," Jake cautioned.

Sam stopped. She was out of smart arguments for taking Jinx off the ranch, but she hadn't mentioned her best reason.

Jake watched her from beneath his hat brim.

"Spit it out," he said finally.

"If Jinx remembers how it feels to run for the joy of it, without being jerked up short, I think he'll be the perfect horse. Besides, Clara wants to race him."

"That claiming race you mentioned," Jake said.

"You remembered," Sam said. She was sort of

amazed. Jake had had plenty on his mind since they'd gone bouncing over the range yesterday and she'd asked him how a claiming race worked.

"Sure," Jake said, as if he'd be dumb not to remember. "And now you want me to back you up when you talk to Brynna."

It wasn't a question, exactly. It took a few seconds for Sam to realize that Jake was making an offer. He agreed with her. He'd face Brynna and tell her so.

"You bet," Sam told him.

Jake sighed. "I was afraid you'd say that."

By the time Brynna emerged from the house and stretched up to hand her a cup of lemonade, Jinx had rested for nearly half an hour.

Sam drained the cup of lemonade. Neither she nor Jinx were dehydrated now, and all she had to do now was explain her plan for restoring Jinx's self-esteem.

As Sam handed her cup back down, Brynna raised an eyebrow in suspicion. "What are you two cooking up?" she asked.

"It's not a big deal," Sam started.

Brynna leaned against the fence as if she had all the time in the world.

"I have this idea for Jinx," Sam said. "If we take him back out on War Drum Flats, where he ran with the Phantom yesterday, and let him run again, he might remember he can have fun moving fast with a rider on his back."

Brynna frowned. She jiggled the latch on the gate.

"After all," Sam said, "Clara wants to race him. I don't know if Dad told you."

Brynna nodded, then motioned Sam to silence.

Was Brynna was worried over what Dad would say? Riders galloped out on the *playa* all the time. She and her best friend Jen raced Ace and Silly about once a week and nothing had ever gone wrong.

Since Brynna hadn't said no yet, Sam bit her lip and waited.

"Jake, what do you think?" Brynna asked.

As much as Sam wished Brynna would just trust her on this, she and Jake had both known Brynna would seek his opinion.

Jake was a little older and a lot more experienced than Sam. But he wasn't saying anything.

Sam signaled Jake with a meaningful stare. He'd agreed to back her up. To do that, he'd have to open his mouth.

"It could work," Jake said.

Don't jump up and down with enthusiasm, Sam thought, shaking her head.

"He's fast, but he's not fresh," Jake added. "Witch could maybe run alongside."

"Okay," Brynna said.

Okay? Sam couldn't believe they'd won so easily.

"She's just going to go out there?" Amelia asked. Her cheeks were bright red. "And ride him across the prairie?"

"Across the *playa*," Brynna corrected gently. "Which is the flat, white bottom of ancient Lake Lahontan . . . but, yes."

Amelia's eyes focused far beyond Brynna and River Bend Ranch. The idea of riding outside a stable's ring, free of fences, made her look dreamy.

Sam wondered if she should tell Amelia how tricky it could be riding the range, but the point of HARP was to allow girls a sense of accomplishment. A dream of riding free might help Amelia set a goal and get there.

"Can I pet him while you're up?" Amelia asked, leaving Crystal's side to stand near Jinx.

"Sure," Sam said.

"I just know you're right," Amelia said as Jinx lowered his chocolate-colored lips to her hand. "About him not wanting to run because he's afraid he'll get in trouble?" She glanced up at Sam and gave a short laugh. "And then he gets in trouble for not running."

Sam nodded. Then Amelia added something that made absolutely no sense at all. "I guess it takes one to know one."

Hawk wings created a whirling shadow on the *playa*.

Sam looked up, then winced at the glare. The hawk vanished in the dazzle of the noon sun directly overhead, but she heard its cry and the whisk of feathers.

Riding at a jog, it had taken half an hour to reach the *playa*. A breeze had sprung up, bringing the scents of hot rocks, sagebrush, and something like berries. Dust swirled between pinion pines on the hillside.

A path that looked like nothing more than a scuff in the dirt ran up that hillside.

Although it was one of the Phantom's getaway trails, nothing moved up there except the pinion branches and dust.

Just ahead, Sam saw Dad's truck pull to a stop. Thank goodness Brynna was driving. She had turned off the highway and onto a dirt road that overlooked the pond at War Drum Flats.

In a flurry of magenta blouse and jeans, Crystal appeared, then leaned against the truck's front fender, using something—maybe a magazine—to fan herself.

It wasn't that hot. Brynna said the high temperature today was supposed to be around eighty degrees. Just the same, Jinx was once more dark with sweat.

As they rode, Jake studied the grulla.

"What?" Sam said.

"Watching him move—" Jake broke off, shaking his head. "For a fit, strong horse, he looks unsure."

"Not in a minute, he won't," Sam said, and her own words catapulted her pulse higher.

Feeling her excitement, Jinx's hooves stuttered on the chalky footing.

"No mustangs today," Sam told Jinx.

She was silly to feel disappointed, but when they'd run together, Jinx and the Phantom had been beautiful.

A tiny, insane voice in her mind was rooting for a match race. That would be asking for trouble, but it would be wonderful to watch.

And if Dad saw it, she'd be dead meat.

"Tell me before you two take off," Jake said. "I'll make Witch hang back 'til you've got him going."

Witch was a Quarter Horse, speedy as a jack-rabbit over short distances. She could probably stay with Jinx for a few minutes, but then his mustang endurance would kick in.

Miles of *playa* stretched before them, level and bare.

Jinx's head flew up as he recognized the possibilities of that open country.

Could this be his home range?

Tonight for homework, Brynna was going to have the girls figure out the coded brand on Jinx's neck. What if he'd come from one of the herds nearby?

All at once, the gelding tensed.

"Now," Sam said. She tightened her seat and urged Jinx forward, but there was another reason for his head to come up. He was going to balk.

"Come on, boy." Sam sighed, then used every muscle to ride as if he were already running. Jinx's head rose even higher.

Somewhere she'd read that a horse couldn't stride beyond the tip of his nose. If that was so, they weren't about to lunge into a gallop.

Still, Jinx hadn't stopped. That was better than last time, in the corral.

Even though his high-kneed prance wasn't what she wanted, Sam was thankful Jinx hadn't frozen into his four-poster balk.

"Hold on." Jake's voice came from over Sam's shoulder.

She glanced back in time to see Witch leap from a jog into a run. So much for the "hanging back" Jake had promised.

As the black mare swept past, Sam understood Jake's strategy. He was hoping Jinx's herd instinct would take over and he'd burst into a run.

"C'mon boy, catch her." Sam leaned low and cheered into the gelding's ears. "You can do it, easy. Catch her!"

The gelding's hammering shamble said he wanted to chase Witch, but he was afraid.

"I won't jerk on your tender mouth," Sam promised.

All at once, Jinx's head moved forward and his legs swept into a gallop. Sam tried to mold her body to the gait, but she was too late.

Sam slammed back in the saddle. Her hat blew from her head and hit the end of the stampede string, tightening around her throat.

But it didn't matter. The gelding swung into a graceful gallop.

It was easy to ride, though the hot wind made it hard to draw a breath. If she could have, Sam thought, she'd be yelling "yippee" as Jinx thundered on, closing the distance to Witch's floating black tail.

Just before he reached the mare, Jinx veered left. Sam shifted her weight, asking him to run alongside Witch instead of heading for the hills.

Never breaking stride, he obeyed. They passed Witch. And the pond. For the first time all year, Sam didn't check for the mustangs' hoof prints in the mud. She was past it too quickly.

A sudden push from Jinx's hindquarters made Sam stay centered as he swerved left again. And then she knew why. Jinx saw the Phantom.

Speeding silver with an ice-white mane, the stallion charged down from the foothills with his mouth agape.

Now, anything could happen.

Sam's stomach dropped. It was one thing to watch the Phantom warn back horses he saw as intruders. It was another thing to be astride one.

Will it matter when he sees me? Sam wondered. The stallion had to know Jinx wasn't alone. A rider and flapping leather gear were never part of a mustang's silhouette.

Then, the stallion was beside them, matching Jinx stride for stride. Nearly a year ago, the Phantom had come upon her as she rode around a herd of cattle at night, and he'd herded Ace, with her aboard, back to his secret valley.

That night, he'd seemed aware that she was Ace's rider.

Not today. Neck lowered, head level, the stallion saw Jinx's speed, not his nearness to the herd, as a challenge. But the Phantom didn't notice Sam at all.

The stallion gloried in his own speed, staying a half length ahead of the grulla's reaching brown-black legs. Puffs of foam blew from Jinx's open mouth. His ears pricked ahead. Gusts of breath sounded over his battering hooves. Once more, Jinx was transformed by running.

Sam imagined the broken heart brand on his shoulder and saw the two halves fusing closed.

Chapter Twelve ∽

 itch was galloping about a length to Jinx's right, working to stay even with Jinx's hindquarters, when Sam heard Jake say something.

"Peel off, Sam."

Careful not to make Jinx shy with Sam in the saddle, Jake didn't shout. He moved his head to one side, indicating she should swerve away from the Phantom.

A quick glance showed Sam that Jake didn't look worried.

Unbelievable! Sam felt her lips turn up in a grin.

The horses were running for the joy of it and so was she. A year ago, she wouldn't have believed she could be riding at a gallop, safely and in control, across Nevada's high desert. But she was.

She let Jinx run a minute more, then slowly and carefully flexed her fingers against the reins.

"Easy," she told Jinx, but she braced for the sliding stop he'd pulled before.

Abruptly, he settled into a jolting trot. Witch stayed alongside him, though the Phantom ran on.

Come back, Sam thought. Her heart yearned after the wild stallion who'd once been her own.

Necks arched and nostrils distended, Witch and Jinx slowed and stopped, but Sam's eyes followed the Phantom.

"Look," she said breathlessly, and Jake didn't have to ask where.

The silver-white stallion swung his muscular shoulders to one side. Then he circled back.

Yes!

The Phantom half reared. His teeth clacked on summer air. Then his front hooves touched down and he shook his mane.

"Wants to play," Jake said. "Like a big dog."

"This boy wants to rest," Sam said, patting Jinx's neck.

Although the grulla's flicking ears said he'd noticed the stallion's antics, Jinx tried to turn his tail toward the Phantom.

"You're not going home yet," she told Jinx.

She'd seen the Phantom for too few minutes in her life. She never knew when it might be the last time, and she refused to stop staring until he disappeared.

With a snort so forceful it carried across the *playa*, the Phantom flipped his ropey forelock away from his eyes. He spun like a cutting horse and galloped back toward the foothills.

His hoofbeats lasted for a full minute.

Looking down, Sam saw her fingers tapping one at a time on the saddle pommel. One, two, three, four. One, two, three, four. Faster and faster, they kept the tempo of the Phantom's gait until his hooves struck almost all at once. And then he was gone.

Amelia, Crystal, Brynna, and Gram were sitting at the kitchen table eating sandwiches frilled with lettuce when Sam and Jake got home.

Sam felt sweaty and dirty, and she smelled like a horse. Not everyone found that appealing.

"I want to ride him," Amelia said as Sam finished washing her hands. "I'd give anything to ride him."

"Obviously, we had a real good time watching you," Brynna said. Though she didn't leave her seat at the table, Brynna looked like she wanted to get up and dance because of Amelia's enthusiasm.

"It could happen," Sam told Amelia.

"Hat," Gram reminded, pointing.

As she removed her hat, Sam blinked back the white alkali dust that showered down and stuck in her lashes. Some of the particles grated until tears started into her eyes.

Her vision was fuzzy, but she was starving. She left her brown Stetson on a hook. Then, drawn by the scent of salami amid all that lettuce, she returned to the kitchen.

"I was wondering when you two would get back." Gram pushed her chair away from the table to assemble their lunches.

"The horses were pretty tired," Sam explained.

"Jinx should enjoy his second grooming of the day, then," Brynna said. "Sort of like a massage."

Gram nodded as she sliced pieces of bread from a homemade loaf, then laid them in a row on the wooden cutting board. She glanced over her shoulder and made an impatient wave at Jake, who still held his black hat, turning it in his hands.

"Jake Ely, of course you'll stay for lunch. You don't have to be asked."

"Yes, ma'am," Jake muttered. "Thanks."

As Sam and Jake sat, Brynna bolted up.

"I'll go get Ace and Popcorn while you finish dessert."

Did Amelia and Crystal pick up Brynna's hints? They dawdled over their sugar cookies, apparently unaware that one of them would get Popcorn and the other Jinx.

Sam didn't know how to feel about that. If she kept working with Jinx, he might be ready for the claiming race. That would make Clara happy, but then Jinx would be gone.

If Amelia or Crystal worked with Jinx, he might be gentler, but unprepared to run next Saturday.

Not sure what to hope for, Sam just bit into her sandwich. She'd have plenty to worry about once she got outside again.

She'd be following Brynna's directions and demonstrating on Ace. That could cause problems. Although she loved her pretty bay mustang with all her heart, he turned tricky when he thought he'd been ignored. She'd have to be on her toes.

"Do horses care about snakes?" Crystal asked suddenly.

A spark of uneasiness sizzled down Sam's back. Why would Crystal want to know?

Jake glanced her way. The same question showed in his eyes.

"They don't like them a bit," Sam answered. "Why, did you see one?"

Crystal made a noncommittal noise.

"Don't expect horses to stomp 'em to death like they do in the movies," Jake told her.

"Never?" Amelia asked, but Crystal talked right over her.

"Brynna said snakes don't come out at night. Is that true?"

"Some do, to hunt," Jake said. "Mostly we see 'em resting on rocks, trying to get warm. They're cold-blooded, you know."

For a minute, there was only the sound of Gram's

knife, slicing through apples.

"Are you thinking about becoming an herpetologist, dear?" Gram asked over her shoulder. "A snake expert," she added when Crystal frowned in confusion.

"No, just curious," Crystal said.

"Brynna should have the horses ready now," Sam said, clearing her place.

Gram kissed her on the cheek and handed her a plastic bowl full of apple chunks.

"For the horses," she said.

Jake rode home with a promise to return in the morning for Sam's written statement.

"You owe me one," Sam grumbled, but she didn't really mind. She'd do anything to help Jake. After all, he was in this predicament because he'd spared Jinx.

"Thanks, Brat," Jake said. "If I keep my license, I'll buy you anything on Clara's menu."

"Don't think I won't collect," Sam shouted after him.

The afternoon passed quietly, with the girls grooming Jinx and Popcorn. It was immediately evident that Amelia, just as she'd said, had been around horses and loved them. It was just as obvious that Crystal was afraid of Popcorn.

"He's a sweet horse," Sam told her. "Just hold your hand completely flat, like this, and offer him the apple. Stop!" she shouted when Crystal's fist, with a bit of apple showing at the top, trembled toward

Popcorn. "If you do that, he can't help but bite your fingers along with the treat."

"Forget it!" Crystal threw the apple on the ground.

Unconcerned, Popcorn stretched to the end of his rope to reach it. Then, chewing, juice running from the corners of his mouth, he looked gratefully at the girl.

"He's thanking you," Sam said.

"He's disgusting," Crystal snapped.

Sam drew a deep breath. Popcorn, with his wise blue eyes and accepting manner, would never qualify as "disgusting."

Crystal was asking for it.

"I'll work with Crystal, shall I?" Brynna said, stepping closer.

"Just in time," Sam said under her breath, then she walked over to Amelia, who'd just finished cleaning Jinx's hooves.

The bespectacled girl gave Jinx's shoulder an admiring pat.

"He's really fast, isn't he?" Amelia asked, tracing her finger over the gelding's heart-shaped brand. "I mean, he doesn't just look that way to me because I haven't been around horses for a while, right?"

Sam recognized the longing in Amelia's eyes. There were people who liked riding and those who loved everything about horses—from the way they shimmered in the sun to the velvety crinkles on their lips. She was pretty sure Amelia fell into the second group.

"He *is* really fast," Sam admitted.

"Could he win that claiming race?" Amelia asked suddenly. "I heard you talking about it and, uh, I read that flier you left on your bed."

Sam didn't call Amelia a sneak, but she wanted to. She was certain she'd slipped the flier under her pillow—not left it on her bed.

"Darton's near here, right?" Amelia asked.

Sam nodded. Did Amelia know that the winning horse in a claiming race would probably go away to a new home?

"I'm feeling kind of sad that Clara wants to enter him in a claiming race," Sam said.

"Why?" Amelia's face returned to this morning's milky paleness.

"It's not really bad," Sam assured her. "But people put a bid on the horse before the race and whoever's bid is highest claims him after the race."

"Claim him? Like buy him?" Amelia sputtered. "But what if you don't want to sell your horse?"

"Then I guess you'd be silly to enter him in a claiming race," Sam said. Suspicion flared in her mind when Amelia avoided meeting Sam's eyes by taking off her glasses and polishing them with the hem of her tee-shirt.

"Then I guess you wouldn't want to enter that white stallion. Brynna said he used to be yours."

"He was," Sam sighed.

Even though it was obvious Amelia was just trying

to distract her, Sam wished she were sitting down by the cottonwoods edging the La Charla River, planning how to race the Phantom. She wanted to look up and see the stallion coming toward her through the shallows. . . .

"Hey, Sam," Amelia said suddenly. "I know we're supposed to wait until the end of the week, but do you think Brynna might let me ride Jinx sooner? I just can't wait."

"Let's get through today," Sam said. "But I wouldn't be surprised. Brynna is pretty cool that way."

After dinner that night, Amelia was elbow-deep in dishwater, grumbling.

"I didn't know there was anyone in America who didn't have a dishwasher," she said. "The hot water steams up my glasses, the detergent makes my hands red, and it's a total waste of time."

"Talk to my Gram," Sam advised her. "She doesn't think they get as clean in a dishwasher."

"I think it's the other way around," Crystal said as she handed Samantha a dried plate.

"Don't tell me," Sam said as she set the plate on a shelf in the pine cupboard.

Amelia had just turned off the water, empathically, when the door to the living room swung open and Brynna came in with a stack of papers.

"Homework time," she said cheerfully.

"No way," Crystal said, throwing the dishtowel

down on the counter. "I don't even do homework during school. Why should I do it in summer?"

Amelia grumbled her agreement until Brynna said, "It's horse homework."

"Really?" Sam asked.

"Sure," Brynna said, giving Sam, Amelia, and Crystal copies of the handout.

Sam considered the page.

JINX'S FREEZE MARK

Use the table below to fill in these blanks:

JINX'S BIRTH DATE: _____

JINX'S HOME RANGE IS IN THIS STATE: _____

KEY TO THE ALPHA ANGLE SYMBOL:

Read each angle in this example to determine the freeze mark number

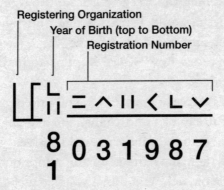

Arizona	Nevada
80001–16000	480001–640000
California	New Mexico
160001–240000	640001–720000
Colorado	Oregon
240001–320000	0–80000
Idaho	Utah
320001–400000	720001–800000
Montana	Wyoming
400001–480000	800001–880000

Sam smiled. This was a first. Usually she felt nervous when faced with a sheet of numbers, but not this time.

By matching the freeze mark on Jinx's neck with this chart, she could learn his age and where he'd come from. This could be exciting.

"I don't get how we're supposed to do this," Amelia said.

"What's a freeze mark?" Crystal asked.

"The Bureau of Land Management—the government agency that rounds up wild horses when it's necessary, then puts them up for adoption—shaves the left side of each wild horse's neck, swabs it with a little alcohol, then presses on a pattern with liquid nitrogen."

Both Amelia and Crystal recoiled, and though Sam knew the process wasn't supposed to be painful, it gave her the creeps, too.

"It's cold, but it doesn't hurt," Brynna insisted, "and it leaves a permanent, unchangeable mark telling the horse's age and home state."

"Who cares about that stuff?" Crystal asked wearily, but Brynna refused to be provoked.

"Lots of people," she said. "And tonight, so do you. Right now," Brynna said, handing each of them a pencil, "the three of you will go outside and copy Jinx's freeze mark. I've already checked it and you won't be able to read the last few digits without reshaving his neck. For now, though, all I want you to do is copy down these."

Brynna tapped her copy of the handout example, pointing out the position of the symbol showing Jinx's year of birth and the first number of the state where he'd been captured.

"Got it," Sam said, eager to unravel the mystery.

"So this will tell us who he really is," Amelia said slowly.

"Actually," Brynna said, "we already know he's a sweet-tempered horse that runs like the wind, but balks when you ask him to do it. Still, the freeze mark will tell us more."

For some reason, Sam was reminded of the talk

she'd had with Brynna on the night before Amelia and Crystal arrived. She'd heard facts about the girls' troubles, but meeting them had told her much more.

Sam pushed the thought aside and asked, "Can we go now?"

Then, they did.

Jinx and Popcorn nickered a welcome as Sam opened the round pen gate.

Sam found she had to divide her attention between Amelia, who rushed into the round pen, and Crystal, who insisted she could do the assignment just fine by peering between the corral's rails from outside.

"You don't know what you're missing," Amelia said as Popcorn nuzzled her pocket, sniffing for a treat.

When Crystal gave a critical huff, Amelia didn't seem to notice.

That's progress, Sam thought, but then she poised her pencil to start copying the freeze mark.

"Hey Jinx, good boy," she crooned to the grulla.

Jinx stood against the far fence, ears pricked to attention. Clearly he was interested, but he wasn't coming any closer.

"Stay back," Sam told Amelia when she started to approach the gelding.

Amelia's eyes widened in surprise. "But why? He's gentle. Brynna said so."

"He's sweet-tempered, but he's had a hard day,"

Sam explained. "Let him relax a little. You can see well enough to write down those lines, right?"

"I guess," Amelia said, giving in.

Looking from the horse to her pad, back and forth, Sam wrote down Jinx's freeze mark.

"Time to call it a day, girls," Brynna called from the porch.

"Just in time," Crystal said, and both Amelia and Sam agreed they'd barely gotten it down, too.

"Before you go," Brynna said, as the girls started for the bunkhouse, "let me tell you to keep your answer secret. Tomorrow there'll be a prize for anyone who's correctly transcribed Jinx's birth date and state of origin."

"What's she think this is, kindergarten?" Crystal mumbled.

Amelia shrugged, but Sam noticed she'd folded her paper in quarters.

Sam let the other girls use the bunkhouse shower first. As they did, she matched the angles with the numbers. Once she had, she thought that Jinx must have found his escape from Clara's coffee shop bittersweet.

The smoky-silver gelding had finally come home.

❖ ❖ ❖

By dawn the next day, Sam was convinced there wasn't a single reason she and Brynna couldn't have a meeting at eight thirty instead of five thirty.

She'd tried to stay awake until Amelia and Crystal had fallen asleep last night, but she'd failed.

Amelia's whispered "no!" had roused her, sometime after midnight, but Sam hadn't asked what they were talking about. Instead, she'd taken comfort in hearing Amelia stand up to Crystal. Then, Sam had rolled over and gone back to sleep.

Now she pulled herself into a sitting position and rubbed her face with both hands. When she dropped her hands into her lap, she thought she saw Amelia's open eyes snap closed.

Sam glanced at Crystal's bunk. The girl was wrapped like a mummy in her covers.

Moving on tiptoe, Sam went to the bathroom sink and threw cold water on her face. Wide awake, she dressed, then she sat on her bunk to pull on her boots. There was no way she was going down that path in socks. She shuddered. She wouldn't sit on a boulder she might be sharing with a rattlesnake, even on a dare.

She picked up her homework and, once outside, Sam sprinted toward the ranch house.

"Are you going to let Amelia ride Jinx before Thursday?" Sam asked once she and Brynna faced each other over hot drinks.

What she really wanted was to ask what she'd won, but she tried to be mature, even though it was just the three of them today. Dad had stayed out all night gathering strays with Pepper and Ross.

"Probably tomorrow," Brynna said. "She's doing great."

"Given their situations," Gram said over the sound of her wire whisk beating froth onto more hot chocolate, "I think both those young ladies are doing just fine. It's only Tuesday, for heaven's sake."

"What are you doing, Gram?" Sam asked. Since Dad and the cowboys were gone, the cups of hot chocolate couldn't be for them.

"She's spoiling those girls. I don't think HARP pictured serving them breakfast in bed," Brynna said in a despairing tone.

"This is not breakfast in bed," Gram insisted. "Just a little cocoa to start the morning off right."

With Blaze bouncing at her heels, Gram opened the door with one hand while the other held the handles of two blue pottery mugs. She bustled out the door, avoiding any more discussion.

"It can't hurt, I suppose," Brynna said. "I'm going to make them shovel manure later today, so it'll balance out."

Sam laughed, but then she remembered Crystal saying Popcorn was disgusting just because he'd drooled a little bit.

"What are we going to do with Crystal?"

"You mean how squeamish she is, and fearful?" Brynna asked.

"Not just that," Sam said. "Last night, I was telling them they had to wear boots when they rode, and I kind of made a big deal about, you know, having a heel so your foot didn't slip through the stirrup and all that, and she refused."

"Well, she's not mounting any horse on this ranch without boots," Brynna said. "It's a safety issue. HARP requires it."

"I know," Sam said. "Do you think she's just being difficult, or is she really afraid of horses?"

"From what I've heard, Crystal isn't afraid of much of anything." Brynna sighed. "I guess we should just be glad she hasn't tried any of the adrenaline junkie stunts I was warned about."

"I guess," Sam said, but then she stopped.

She listened.

From out in the yard, had Gram called her name?

Eyes wide with dread, Brynna stood. She was around the kitchen table and moving toward the door when Gram shouted again and Blaze began to bark.

Chapter Thirteen ∾

"Crystal's missing," Gram shouted from the middle of the yard.

Brynna turned toward Sam as she started out the door.

"Call Sheriff Ballard," she said.

"But why?" Sam asked. She'd seen Brynna deal with wild horse rustlers who ended up in prison. Surely she could handle Crystal.

Amid the confusion, Brynna didn't seem to hear her.

"Will you get down!" Brynna said, impatiently, pushing Blaze away when he jumped up at her, still barking.

"Sam, was she still there when you left the bunk-house?" Gram asked as she came closer.

"Yes, I'm sure—" Sam broke off. "No, I'm not. I thought I saw her, but she was all bundled up. I guess she could have arranged blankets to look like it was her."

Sam spotted Amelia sprinting down the sun-flower path as if she expected a snake to whip around her ankle if she didn't hurry.

"We'd better ask her." Sam pointed.

"I tried," Gram said. "She's being stubborn. We'd best get started without her help."

"I'll talk to Amelia," Brynna said coldly. "Sam, call the sheriff."

This time, Sam didn't question Brynna's instructions.

Sam's hands shook as she held the telephone receiver and stared at the neon green list of emergency phone numbers posted next to it.

By the time she talked her way past the county switchboard, Sam was frustrated and flushed.

As she waited on hold for the sheriff's office, Sam wondered if Brynna would stop her from strangling Crystal.

This might be the last time HARP trusted River Bend Ranch to run the program, since Crystal had just proven they hadn't kept close enough track of her.

Crystal obviously didn't care about anyone except

herself, but Amelia! How could she do this to them when the HARP program had brought Amelia together with Jinx?

Most of all, Sam was mad at herself for sleeping through Crystal's escape.

She slammed her fist against her jean leg.

"Come on, come *on*," she muttered into the telephone's mouthpiece.

Finally the sheriff answered.

"Ballard."

"This is Samantha Forster at River Bend Ranch. One of the HARP girls is missing," Sam blurted.

"Why didn't you dial 911?" Sheriff Ballard snapped.

Sam sucked in a breath. Of course. That would have saved lots of time. Why hadn't she thought of it?

"I, uh, didn't think it was an emergency," she said.

Then Sheriff Ballard dumped an avalanche of other questions on her, and each one embarrassed Sam more because she didn't know the answers.

What was Crystal's last name? How tall was she? Who had seen her last? When? What had she been wearing? Had she ever run away before?

"Yes!" Sam answered, glad to finally know an answer.

"Did she have access to a vehicle?"

"She's only going into eighth grade," Sam began. Then she remembered Crystal had been arrested for joyriding in a stolen car. "She had access, but—" Sam pulled back the curtain to see Gram's car and both trucks parked where they belonged. "All our vehicles are here."

"Tell you what, Samantha," Sheriff Ballard said, and Sam realized he hadn't just been sitting at his desk when she heard a car start. "I'm on my way out to River Bend, but since she's pulled this before, I'll keep Search and Rescue on standby."

The screen door creaked and Sam looked up.

"Tell him we'll start looking from our end," Brynna shouted as she grabbed a jacket from the hook by the front door.

Sam repeated the message to the sheriff.

"Leave someone there in case she comes back on her own," he cautioned.

"He said to leave someone here—" Sam began after she'd hung up.

Gram had just come into the kitchen. Amelia followed her. Red-rimmed eyes showed behind her glasses. After one quick glance Sam's way, Amelia looked down.

"You two will be riding faster than I'd like, so I'll stay here with Amelia," Gram said. "I've got Popcorn and Jinx up in the round pen if you want to take them."

Surprised, Brynna said, "Thanks, Grace. When—?"

"I woke up early—Blaze was scratching at the door, crazy to go out. Guess I know why now—" Gram shook her head. "It never crossed my mind that one of the girls would leave. But I suppose there's plenty of blame to go around. We're all new at this.

"At any rate, I like being in the pasture at daybreak, so I figured I'd save you the trouble of catching them. Good thing I did. Of course, Ace is just green with jealousy."

Sam could hear her bay gelding neighing. Another equine voice joined his. Dark Sunshine, she thought, and a jolt of anxiety made her worry about Tempest. The foal shouldn't be surrounded by tension she couldn't understand.

Sam followed Brynna out the door.

A glance toward the ten-acre pasture showed her Ace, gleaming red-gold in the rising sun.

On the porch behind her, Sam heard footsteps. Then she heard sniffing. Amelia was crying, but Sam was too angry to comfort her.

As Sam hurried after Brynna, Amelia followed.

Brynna stood with one hand on the gate of the round pen as she asked, "Do you want to take Jinx?"

"He's the fastest," Amelia insisted.

Sam shook her head. "I can't count on him."

Amelia blushed. "He just needs a chance."

"Too much is at stake if he blows it," Sam told her. "If I have to deal with his balking, or if I get thrown, I've just created another problem."

Amelia's hands tangled in front of her. Inside the round pen, Brynna clucked her tongue at Popcorn, about to lead him out.

Sam knew she should be getting the tack instead of talking to Amelia. She turned toward the barn.

"I didn't know she was really going to do it!" Amelia said.

Sam whirled back. "No, but if we lose the HARP program, it's your fault!"

"Samantha, you're out of line," Brynna said over the sound of Amelia's weeping. "I'm the adult in charge. I should have known better than to—there's no time for this now. Bring me the tack, then go get a horse."

She should have known better than to trust me sleeping in the bunkhouse, Sam thought as she took down Popcorn's and Ace's bridles. That's what Brynna had been about to say.

Sam hurried even faster, struggling under the weight of the two saddles.

Sam had reached Brynna and Popcorn when Blaze began yapping excitedly and Jake, driving his mother's damaged Honda, bumped over River Bend's bridge.

"What now?" Brynna said as she slapped the saddle blanket on Popcorn and shifted it into position, all the while watching Jake.

"He asked me to write a statement about the accident for him. It's in the bunkhouse," Sam said.

"Jake can get it himself. Just tell him where you left it," Brynna ordered. "We should have been saddled up and out of here by now and you still have to catch Ace."

"Right," Sam said, then sprinted toward the ten-acre pasture.

Ace was rubbing against the gate when Sam reached it. He'd be easy to halter. Ace had an instinct for when to play games and when to cooperate.

As she came closer, Ace tossed his head in excitement, showing the white star that lay beneath his black forelock.

"You're my best boy," Sam crooned to the horse, but when he stared over her head, Sam looked back, too.

Crystal stood beside the Honda with Jake.

Hooves struck the fence behind her as Sam hurried toward them. Poor Ace would have to wait a little longer.

Arms folded and tucked against her ribs, Crystal faced Brynna.

"I just needed a ride to Las Vegas," Crystal claimed.

Brynna blinked, ignored the fact that Las Vegas was about seven hundred miles away, and considered the girl carefully.

"You want to go home?" Brynna asked. She was usually such an understanding person, Sam was shocked by her strict tone.

"Not home, just Las Vegas."

"And you thought Jake would give you that ride?" Brynna asked.

"Why shouldn't he?" Crystal's voice quavered.

Her hands covered her eyes for a minute. "Besides, I didn't know it was him until he pulled over. I was in the car before I recognized him." Crystal's hands dropped away from her eyes and all of her vulnerability fell away, too. "He wouldn't help me."

Crystal glared at Jake with a venom that told its own story.

Sam imagined Crystal begging Jake to keep driving south. His stubborn refusal would have made Crystal furious.

"She was hitchhiking, about a half mile on down the road." Jake nodded toward Darton.

"We won't discuss the danger involved," Brynna began.

"Nothing happened. I can do anything I want and nothing ever happens," Crystal sneered. "It's just like your rattlesnakes. Scary stories to keep kids in line."

Silence hung around them for a full minute, but Sam recognized Brynna's fury. Crystal must have, too.

"Hey, he grabbed my arm," Crystal accused. She pointed at Jake, then pushed at her sleeve, searching for a bruise.

Brynna's complexion matched her red hair, but she was struggling for the words of a professional.

"Thank you, Jake," Brynna said.

"*Thank* you?" Crystal roared.

"Shall I call Sheriff Ballard and tell him we found her?" Sam asked.

"No. Let him keep coming."

"Oh, right," Crystal hooted with fake laughter. "Like I'll be afraid of some cow county sheriff!"

"No," Brynna said quietly. "Like I want an official record of this. Go sit on the porch."

Defiance flared in Crystal's pale blue eyes, but only for a second. Then she saw Amelia watching from the porch.

"Yes ma'am," Crystal said in a mocking tone, then sauntered away.

"You are a lifesaver." Brynna gripped Jake's forearm.

Embarrassed, he shrugged. "I did grab her arm. The car was moving and she opened the door to jump."

Sam pictured Jake's strong right hand, his roping hand, reaching over to clamp on Crystal's arm. Then, stubbornly and silently, he'd keep driving.

Giggles fought to escape Sam's lips. She covered her mouth to smother them. Laughter would be totally inappropriate right now, but she couldn't help thinking that if Jake had been Crystal's big brother, she'd be less of a pain.

"You're not in trouble, Jake," Brynna assured him.

"Yeah," he said on a long sigh. "I am." He glanced pointedly at his mother's car. "It's either pay to have it fixed—which I can't do without touching my savings—or fix it myself."

Jake's eyes scanned the ten-acre pasture and the hitching rail where Popcorn stood alone. "You get rid of Jinx?"

"He's in the round pen," Sam said.

Sure Jake was having a run of bad luck, but he couldn't blame it on Jinx.

Jake nodded and Sam was about to go retrieve her written account of the accident when Sheriff Ballard arrived. Before he was even out of the car, he'd taken in their relaxed demeanor.

"Is one of them our runaway?" he asked, nodding toward the porch.

"The dark-haired girl," Brynna said. "Jake found her out on the highway, trying to hitchhike to Las Vegas."

"Dangerous business, hitchhiking," the sheriff said. "These kids don't think. Even out here, you never know who's passing through. I'll go have a word with her."

"My curiosity might kill me," Sam whispered, staring after Sheriff Ballard.

"Mine, too, but it's better if we stay here," Brynna said.

Jake shifted his weight from boot to boot, then darted a glance at Sam.

"I'll go get that thing I wrote," she said.

She tried to eavesdrop as she jogged off toward the bunkhouse, but she only heard a fragment of conversation.

"You talk to me, not her." Sheriff Ballard's tone said he meant business.

Before she started down the path to the bunkhouse, Sam studied each boulder individually. No snakes.

"Probably couldn't stand the craziness around here," Sam mumbled to herself.

Inside the quiet bunkhouse, Sam found her statement and returned—just as carefully—to give it to Jake.

The girls were nowhere in sight. Sam guessed they were inside the house, since Sheriff Ballard stood talking to Brynna.

Jake stood off a few paces and his turned back gave them some privacy.

When Sam reached Jake, she gestured him to keep his voice down. She had to know what Brynna and the sheriff were saying.

"Our girl Crystal's been through this before," the sheriff said. "Knows runaway is a juvenile status offense, that it wouldn't be a crime if she was eighteen, and keeps saying she needs to get to Las Vegas. Won't say why, and she swears she's not trying to get home, but I'll bet if we check, she's tried to get home before."

Sam felt a sudden prickling of tears. She didn't like Crystal, but she understood her, a little bit.

Her own dad hadn't sent her away after Mom had died, but he had made her live in San Francisco with

Aunt Sue after the accident. Even though she'd known it was for her own good, she'd resented it.

It would hurt a lot more if she'd believed Dad had been sending her away for punishment.

"Something's not right," Brynna said.

"Horse coming." Jake's voice crowded out the other conversation. He stared toward the range. "Wyatt and the hands due back this morning?"

"I don't know," Sam hissed, then made a flat-palmed gesture for Jake to keep his voice down.

"—put a call in to someone. I mean, Crystal doesn't even like horses," Brynna said.

"Imagine that," the sheriff joked, but Brynna went on talking.

"HARP kids go through a rigorous screening process. They want to be here. It's supposed to be the best of all possible second chances."

"And she's throwin' it away." Sheriff Ballard shook his head. He gave Brynna a sort of salute before turning toward his vehicle. As he did, he caught Sam's eye and his official demeanor changed.

"Samantha, how's that grulla doin'?"

"Great!" she answered.

"He has a few rough edges," Brynna corrected. "But he's still here."

"Had a chance to see if he's as fast as that cowboy said?" Sheriff Ballard asked.

"Faster." Brynna's voice had a teasing edge as she motioned the sheriff to walk toward the round pen.

Yes, Sam thought. If HARP wouldn't buy Jinx for the program, maybe Sheriff Ballard would. That would keep Clara from putting him in the claiming race, and the horse would have a good home.

And she'd still get to see him sometimes.

Sam's excitement was bubbling up when hooves clattered on the bridge.

It was Dad. He rode Jeepers-Creepers, their only Appaloosa, into the ranch yard. The horse was wet and wild-eyed and Dad didn't look happy.

Chapter Fourteen ❧

Dad slowed Jeepers to a jog, but he didn't stop the Appaloosa until he was within a few feet of them.

"Somethin' goin' on?" he asked, swinging down from the snorting horse.

"We're all fine," Brynna assured him. "Crystal ran away, but Jake caught her before she got very far."

Dad's shoulders sank about two inches. He'd been worried, Sam realized.

"We were bringing in strays when I saw the black and white," Dad nodded toward the sheriff's vehicle. "Thought there mighta been an accident."

"Me showin' up has that effect on people," Sheriff Ballard said. "But everything's okay. Those two girls could use a watchful eye, though."

"And it's only Tuesday," Brynna said with a sigh.

"You rethinkin' your enthusiasm for this project?" Dad asked.

Brynna shook her head so hard her braid whipped over her shoulder and swung partway around her neck.

"Absolutely not." Brynna's hands perched on her hips and she lifted her chin to meet Dad's gaze. "It will be worth it."

Their stare-off lasted until Sheriff Ballard broke it up. "We were just talking about that grulla horse of Clara's."

"Better get your bid in on that claiming race," Dad suggested. "You used to ride rodeo. He couldn't show you any tricks you haven't already seen."

Sam drew a deep breath. Dad hadn't seen Jinx's spectacular balk. Still, if Sheriff Ballard had been a rodeo rider, he'd know what to do.

"It's tempting," Sheriff Ballard said, watching Jinx touch noses with Blaze through the round pen's fence rails.

"And you've got about an acre and a half out at your place, don't you?" Brynna asked.

"Thing is, I'd want him for Search and Rescue. He'd have to be smart, and okay around tracking dogs. He'd need to be surefooted on all terrain and willing to try new things. If he gets scared, he can't bolt. Standing still is the required response."

Sam laughed as she recalled the gelding's four-poster balk when he feared moving into a gallop.

"No problem," she said. Jake and Brynna smiled, too.

"Am I missing something?" Dad's tone said he didn't like being left out.

"Jinx gets a little balky when you ask him to run," Brynna said. "Our theory is, he had a novice rider who was afraid to gallop."

"I think he—or she—jerked Jinx up hard and maybe even hurt his mouth," Sam added. "Now, he's not sure what to do when you ask him to run."

"You've been riding him?" Dad asked.

Something in Dad's tone made Sam careful. Ever since her accident, he'd worried she'd have another one.

"Yes," Sam answered, then braced herself.

When Dad only nodded and said, "Sounds like you might be on the right track," Sam was amazed.

"I'm going to get on my way and leave you folks to your business." Sheriff Ballard nodded toward the house, confirming Sam's guess that the girls were inside with Gram. "Don't hesitate to call if you need anything else."

Sheriff Ballard left in a chorus of "thank yous" and Jake drove after him, heading for town. After he dropped off his insurance paperwork, he and his buddy Darrell planned to repair the dent in Mrs. Ely's car.

"Guess I'll switch horses, then go back out and help the boys settle those steers," Dad said. He was rubbing the back of his neck as he often did when he felt awkward or uneasy.

"Is something wrong, Dad?" Sam asked.

"Honey, my heart froze when I saw the sheriff's car speeding down the highway, headed for my home," Dad said, looking a little embarrassed. "Nothing could have stopped me from coming to check on my family."

A lump formed in Sam's throat, making it hard to swallow. Dad didn't talk about feelings much. It touched her when he did.

She and Brynna hugged Dad harder than usual, then went into the kitchen.

Sam expected dead silence and a feeling that punishment was about to descend.

Instead, she saw Amelia eating a sundae. Scoops of vanilla ice cream drizzled with chocolate were mounded in a clear glass dish.

"Hey," Sam said. "What did I miss?"

"Turning in your homework," Gram said.

"I put it somewhere," Sam said, looking around the kitchen. It seemed like it had been a long time since she'd walked in with it at five thirty this morning.

"I suppose, if you and Crystal can write down the correct answers, that would count."

"Great," Sam said, reaching for the pad of paper Gram kept by the telephone.

"Give me one, too," Crystal said, then added, "Please."

"Oh, let's make it an oral test," Gram said. "Crystal, what was Jinx's birth year?"

Crystal swallowed audibly, then managed, "1998?"

"Absolutely," Gram said. "And Sam, his home state?"

"Nevada," Sam said.

"You're both right," Gram said, and then lavished Sam's sundae with chocolate and nuts and Crystal's with butterscotch and marshmallow creme.

Amelia licked her spoon, then looked at Sam with a sheepish smile.

"Grace is going to tell us a story. You know, like when you're a little kid and your teacher read to you after lunch." Amelia shrugged as if she was more excited than she thought she should be.

This whole morning was getting weirder by the second, Sam thought. It was odd, hearing Amelia call Gram by her first name, but Gram must have given her permission. It was even stranger that the girls were getting stories and sundaes when they'd messed up so badly.

What had happened to the consequences that came down on her when she made mistakes? Sam shot Brynna a questioning look but didn't ask. Yet.

"We were talking about Jinx," Gram explained, "and I thought of a story that might apply to that grulla visitor of ours. It's supposed to be taken from a Chinese folktale."

"A Chinese folktale and a Nevada mustang. This, I've got to hear." Brynna pulled out a chair and settled in.

"Once, a farmer had a horse," Gram began. "He used it for everything—riding, plowing, entertaining his children—and then one day, his horse ran away. All his neighbors pitied his bad luck, but the farmer asked, 'How do you know it's not really good luck?'

"Of course, his neighbors thought he was just making the best of a bad situation, but sure enough, two days later, the farmer's horse returned. Running alongside him was a beautiful, spirited mare.

"The farmer's neighbors congratulated him on his good luck, but the farmer looked over each shoulder, appearing worried. 'How do you know it's good luck?'

"The farmer was right to ask, because two days later, the farmer's son was riding the new mare when she bucked, threw him off, and he broke his leg."

Gram paused, looking preoccupied for a minute. Sam almost laughed. She knew Gram used this stalling technique to build suspense.

"Yeah, so then what?" Crystal asked.

"Of course, all of the farmer's neighbors commiserated. How sad, they said, that the farmer would have to do all his work alone, since his son had the bad luck to break his leg. Although the farmer felt sorry for his son, he waited to see what would come of this apparent misfortune.

"Sure enough, good luck came, once more, out of bad. Two weeks later, all the young men of the village were ordered to join the emperor's army. All of them, that is, except for the farmer's son. Because he had a broken leg, he didn't have to go." Gram took a breath and looked at the four of them. "The end."

"So, what does it mean?" Crystal said.

"It's philosophical," Amelia said, seriously.

Crystal looked at her as if she were nuts. For the first time, Sam found herself agreeing with Crystal. Even though she earned A's in English and usually understood the themes of stories, she wasn't sure what Amelia meant by "philosophical."

"I'd guess it's just an observation on how often what seems like bad luck, turns out to be good luck," Brynna mused. "And vice versa, of course."

Sam decided she'd have to think about the story. She had a feeling there was some truth in it.

"That's too deep for me," Crystal said.

"I'll give you an example," Brynna said. Her head tilted to one side and her eyes sparkled.

Uh-oh, Sam thought, Crystal had better watch out. Maybe she wouldn't have to ask Brynna about those consequences after all.

"All morning, I've been thinking what bad luck it was that Sam didn't wake up when you were sneaking out of the bunkhouse —" Brynna began.

"And now you think it's bad luck that I'm back, right?" Crystal said.

"Of course not," Brynna said. "I'm thinking it's good luck that I have to punish you, because now that mountain of firewood behind the barn will get restacked."

"By me?" Crystal asked. She looked at her hands as if they were already dirty and pricked with slivers.

"By you and Amelia," Brynna amended.

"But I didn't do anything!" Amelia gasped as Crystal sat back with a surprised laugh.

"Exactly! Sometimes *doing something* is required." Brynna stood and headed outside.

Amelia trailed after her, still protesting. "But I didn't make her sneak out and go hitchhiking."

Crystal rushed after them, too, probably hoping she wouldn't lose Amelia's help. Sam followed closely, fingers crossed that there'd be no part for her in Brynna's plan.

"No, Amelia, you didn't make Crystal go," Brynna agreed. "But you didn't try to stop her. If she'd been hit by a car as she stood out there on the highway, wouldn't you have felt guilty?"

"I guess," Amelia said.

"You guess? Gee thanks," Crystal snapped.

"So," Brynna said. "Because actions have consequences, you got ice cream for doing your homework. Because you made a big mistake, after we've worked the horses and had lunch, you two will stack firewood."

"I don't know how," Amelia complained.

"Sam will be glad to explain," Brynna said.

Sam waited a second, hoping there was no more to Brynna's request. Then, she recited the directions Dad had given her whenever they'd stacked firewood together.

"You're supposed to stack it so that a mouse can run through, but a cat can't follow," Sam told them.

Brynna flashed her a smile, but Amelia stayed quiet and Crystal asked, in a surly tone, "How hard can that be?"

As the sun rose higher and the morning grew warmer, Amelia and Crystal reviewed what they'd learned of haltering and grooming horses.

When Brynna instructed them on how to saddle and bridle Popcorn and Jinx, Amelia was in heaven.

She eased the bit into Jinx's mouth and bent his silky ears so that she could settle the leather headstall behind them.

When she finished, the grulla rubbed his forehead on Amelia's shirt so hard, she staggered back a step, but she took the gesture as a pledge of friendship.

"We're going to be such a good team," Amelia leaned against Jinx, one arm slung over his neck. "Sam, he doesn't think he can do anything right, so he's afraid to try. But I know just how he feels, and he can tell."

"You know just how he feels?" Sam repeated.

Amelia's mouth opened and her eyebrows rose, as if she were surprised by her own honesty. Then she stroked Jinx's shoulder and explained.

"My older sister Mandy is perfect. Straight A's, an incredible gymnast, and she not only plays the cello, she writes her own music!"

"That's amazing," Sam said.

"That's what everybody says," Amelia replied. "The worst part is that most of my teachers have had Mandy, too. Some of them even slip and call me Mandy. I hate that, because they expect . . ." Amelia's voice trailed off and she shook her head before continuing.

"Anyway, we're good at different things, but no one sees that. Not my parents or my teachers. They expect me to screw up. So why should I even try?"

Sam didn't know how to answer, but she'd bet the perfect Mandy didn't love horses.

"Have your parents ever seen you ride?" Sam asked.

Amelia looked startled, as if Sam had uncovered a secret. "I don't think it would make any difference."

"I bet it would," Sam said. "Mikki, the girl who piloted our HARP program, couldn't believe how excited her mother was when she saw her ride Popcorn. Maybe your parents can come watch you ride on Friday."

"They won't fly in from New Mexico," Amelia said. "Besides, my dad thinks doing anything I want him to do is, like, giving in to me. He says I've got to earn their trust back."

Sam thought for a moment. Amelia had probably deserved her punishment, but her dad would have to be awfully hard-hearted not to let her be around horses again once he saw how much she loved them.

"I have an idea," Sam said. "I'll take some pictures of you with Jinx, and you can take them home with you."

"Yeah," Amelia said in a distracted voice. "I guess that might work."

After lunch Sam supervised the stacking of firewood.

"Wear these," she said, handing scarred leather gloves to the girls. "And don't grab anything you can't see."

"Oh goody, more snake stories," Crystal said.

Sam ignored the girl's taunt. "Dad and Ross checked the woodpile yesterday, but snakes like shady places where they think they'll find mice to eat."

They'd already begun stacking the wood when Brynna showed up with an empty feed sack.

"What's in there?" Sam asked.

"Nothing yet, but I've been noticing that there are an awful lot of nails scattered around the ranch yard. It's a miracle no one's had a flat tire."

It made sense, Sam thought. Last fall there'd been a fire. Many boards had burned completely and only nails had been left from the bunkhouse and parts of the barn which had had to be rebuilt.

"If you run across any, just put them into the sack," Brynna said.

"What for?" Crystal asked. "Are you paying us for every one we find? A dollar each, maybe?"

Brynna smiled at Crystal as if she were a silly little girl. "Your reward will be that warm glow you feel from doing a good deed."

Crystal moaned and rolled her eyes, but Sam was almost sure Crystal was hiding a smile at Brynna's sarcasm.

Then Brynna turned to Amelia.

"Grace said you called home this morning."

Sam watched Amelia. Why hadn't Amelia mentioned the call when they'd been talking about her parents?

Amelia looked uncomfortable, but she nodded. "You were getting ready to go look for Crystal, and my cell doesn't work out here. Grace said it would be okay."

"I think it's fine." Brynna sounded pleased as she handed Amelia the feed sack. "Crystal, you can call home, too, if you want."

"No way. For my dad, no news is good news."

"Oh, now—" Brynna began.

"Look," Crystal said, "he doesn't talk to me since my mom died. We don't have little conversations where we work things out." Crystal shot Sam a glare.

"The only time he pays attention is when he gets a call from school or my parole officer. Then he yells at me and sends me to some treatment program for wayward teens. He won't take me back 'til they say they can't keep me any longer."

Sam held her breath, trying not to react to the news that Crystal had been in so much trouble, she even had a parole officer.

"Your choice," Brynna said, simply. "Sam, once you get the girls started on this, I don't see why you can't spend a few minutes with Tempest."

"Thanks," Sam said.

Everyone who knew mustangs had told Sam that the frisky black filly needed to be handled daily. With Dark Sunshine for a mother and the Phantom for a sire, Tempest had the bloodlines to become smart and spirited. It would be best if she had a human to love, too.

Crystal took off the bulky leather gloves. She was wrapping a ponytail holder around her thick hair, and Sam noticed her hands were shaking.

"If what you say is true," Sam began, "maybe your dad would enjoy getting a normal call. He might like it if you, you know, just called to say hi."

Amelia took a stride closer to Crystal, backing her up as if she'd been criticized.

"Yeah, right!" Amelia flung the feed sack down for emphasis. "How can you give her advice? You've got this perfect cowboy-movie dad and cute, understanding mom. And this healthy fresh-air ranch. You don't know what you're talking about."

Sam took a deep breath and held it until her lungs burned. "Brynna's my stepmother. My real mom's dead. And if I don't know what I'm talking about, I'm not the only one."

Sam crossed her arms. She'd probably made a mistake dragging her own life into this conversation, but she didn't see how it could make things worse.

Surprise flashed over both girls' faces, but Crystal recovered first.

"Your dad didn't send you away no matter how brave you were after your mom died, did he?"

Brave? Is that what Crystal thought she was being by jumping off a roof and stealing a car?

"And he doesn't keep sending you away no matter how many times you come home, does he?"

Sam shook her head. It would break her heart if he did.

"And he doesn't take away everything you care about, no matter how you try to please him, does he?" Amelia added.

Sam felt trapped. These girls needed an expert to answer their questions, and she wasn't it.

"My dad's not perfect either, but this week isn't about him and me. I can't change things for you," Sam said. "But if you do well here, maybe stuff will get better."

Amelia nodded. When Crystal shrugged, a sudden

flash of understanding hit Sam.

Crystal really was afraid of horses, but she was trying to prove her bravery to her dad. That's why she'd fought to be in the HARP program.

"Would your dad be proud if you learned to ride?" Sam asked her.

Crystal started to nod, then sucked in a breath.

"It doesn't matter," Crystal snapped.

Sam sighed. Horses really were so much easier than humans. Still, she tried once more to make them excited.

"Well, what matters now is getting this wood stacked," she said. "Because Brynna said that if it's done, after dinner tonight she's going to let you two mount up, two whole days early."

Chapter Fifteen ❧

$\mathcal{O}$nce the girls' grumbling had tapered off and they were working at a steady pace, Sam decided it was safe to go visit Tempest.

"Watch for snakes," Sam cautioned as she walked toward the barn.

"And dragons and vampires and . . ."

Crystal added more mythical creatures, as if rattlesnakes weren't real, but Sam stopped listening.

Dark Sunshine and her filly had chosen the shade of their stall instead of the bright pasture.

"Good idea, girls," she said as she entered the cool darkness. "It's much nicer in here."

Sunny greeted Sam with a nicker, which made

her smile. This was why she preferred the company of horses.

She talked to the mare for a minute before slipping into the stall. Once inside, Sam bolted the door behind her.

Dark Sunshine watched with interest as Sam worked her way around the stall wall to the far corner.

Already the smells of oats, straw, and leather were relaxing Sam. She didn't mind being patient as she waited for Tempest's curiosity to get the better of her.

Since birth, the long-legged black filly had shown curiosity toward people. Sam's plan was to wait until the foal made a habit of coming to her for pats and scratches, then she'd slip on the tiny leather halter Dad had given her for a birthday gift.

"Hey Tempest," Sam called. "Come here, baby."

As soon as Sam held out her hand, Tempest took a few steps forward.

Tempest glanced back at her mother, seeking permission. When Dark Sunshine lipped the straw underfoot, Tempest took a few more steps.

Finally, the filly extended her neck as far as it would go. Three feet of air still lay between her ebony nose and Sam's fingertips.

Sam rippled her fingers. Tempest's ears tipped forward, but when she realized the flicking fingers made no sound, she ventured a few steps closer to see how they'd taste. As her lips touched Sam's fingers, Tempest made slight sucking movements. It tickled and Sam had to bite her lip to keep from giggling.

With a tiny snort, Tempest raised her muzzle to Sam's face, and Sam decided that was a good time to give Tempest a delicate scratch behind the ears. The filly flinched, but she didn't move away.

Her dark eyes watched Sam carefully, but she wasn't worried enough to let something that felt so good end just yet.

"That's it," Sam crooned. "What a good baby. We'll do this for a couple more days and then I'll try on your pretty halter. Dad made it just for you."

Both horses' heads swung toward the barn door at the sound of loud voices.

"Leave it alone!"

"I'm just going to catch it."

"Crystal, it could be poisonous!"

Sam dashed for the stall door. Each step lasted forever, as if she dragged her boots through knee-deep honey.

She wished she hadn't left the girls alone.

She prayed Crystal had better judgment than she'd shown so far.

Startled by Sam's sudden movement, Dark Sunshine bolted forward.

"Easy, girl!" Sam tried to soothe the mare, then

realized she'd shouted.

Oh, please let someone else be out there. Brynna and Gram were in the house. Maybe they'd heard.

Sunny's eyes rolled, showing white rims, but Sam put a hand on her shoulder.

"You're fine," she said.

Would it be safer to go in front of the buckskin or behind her? Sam's mind spun, calculating risks.

"Gotcha!" Crystal's voice sent the mare wheeling toward the barn pasture.

Swirling straw and dust blinded Sam as the mare and foal disappeared.

Sam made it through the stall door. With a quick swipe, she shot the bolt closed and headed for the woodpile.

She could hardly believe what she saw.

Crystal held the brown snake by the middle of its body. Both ends thrashed, constantly reforming in S shapes.

Crystal's face wore an expression of victory. And revulsion.

Sam approached slowly, afraid to shout for help. Could noise provoke the snake to strike?

It was already trying to attack Crystal. Fighting its captor the only ways it could, the snake made a sound that could have been hissing, or the whir of rattles on its tail.

Even in Crystal's hand, the desperate snake tried

to coil, but its writhing didn't bring it close enough to bite.

"Get me the sack," Crystal croaked, and for the first time Sam glanced at Amelia.

Amelia stood just steps away. Her body angled back from her planted boots and her hands were thrust out as if warding off the snake. From one hand, a gunnysack dangled.

"No," Amelia whispered, but Crystal didn't seem to hear.

"I can't wait to tell my dad I caught a snake. Just hold that sack open."

As Crystal wobbled closer to Amelia, the snake renewed its struggle. The sight shook Amelia from her horrified trance.

"No!" Amelia shouted. Then she tossed the sack away. "Put it down, Crystal."

"Just open your hand and drop the snake," Sam said quietly.

Crystal didn't seem to hear. As she stared at the snake, so did Sam.

Was it a rattlesnake? Its brown and beige markings were right, but its swinging tail was a blur. Was the end of its tail round or pointed? That single detail could mean the difference between life and death.

"It'll crawl away, if you just drop it," Sam insisted.

Still, Crystal didn't react. Was she imagining her father calling this "bravery"? Couldn't she see the difference between courage and foolhardiness?

"You're scaring it, and it's going to bite you." For the first time, Amelia sounded impatient, not scared.

"Shut up," Crystal said.

Maybe Amelia had heard those words one time too many. Before Sam could stop her, the bespectacled girl darted forward and gave Crystal's wrist a violent swat.

The snake should have been grateful, Sam thought, but it fell at the same time that Amelia's hand hit Crystal's. For one awful minute, the snake's mouth hit and hung onto Amelia's hand.

"Brynna!" Sam yelled. "Gram! Help!"

Frantic barking greeted Sam's shouts. Hadn't Brynna warned that snakes were more dangerous to dogs than humans, because dogs put their tender noses right down in striking range?

"Keep Blaze back!" Sam screamed.

Without turning toward the house, Sam heard Gram gasp, "Oh lands, it must be a snake."

It seemed to take forever for Amelia to shake the reptile loose from her right hand, but finally she did.

As the snake plopped on the dirt and went weaving away, Sam got a good look at it. Its tail was smooth and pointed, not bumpy with rattles.

She was almost certain it wasn't a rattlesnake. Almost.

"I didn't mean to!" Crystal looked around frantically. "I was going to keep it in the sack."

Sam ignored her and moved closer to Amelia. The girl's face looked no paler than usual, but she gripped her right wrist, hard.

"His jaws were like—*grinding*," Amelia pronounced the words with slow precision.

"You picked a fine time to stand up to Crystal," Sam teased, and then she pressed her lips closed. She sounded like Jake. Or Dad.

Amelia laughed faintly, and swayed against her.

"Don't pass out on me," Sam ordered.

"And let go of that wrist." Brynna stood beside them now.

"It didn't look like a rattlesnake," Sam told her at once.

Brynna nodded that she'd heard.

"Since we can't be sure, don't hold onto your wrist that way," she repeated to Amelia. "Your grip acts as a tourniquet and that's the last thing we want."

When Brynna moved to loosen Amelia's fingers, she wore a calm and competent expression, but Sam would bet Brynna's heart was beating just as madly as hers.

"What's a person have to do to get some sympathy around here?" Amelia asked in a barely audible—but amused—tone.

"You guys are sick!" Crystal accused. "I'm going to call 911."

"Good idea," Sam said.

Brynna helped Amelia sit down. She held the hand level. She and Gram squatted to examine the bite.

"No fang marks," Brynna said, exhaling. "It barely broke the skin."

It made Sam feel dizzy, just looking down on the three of them, but the bite didn't look serious. On the web of skin between Amelia's thumb and forefinger, Sam saw what looked like tiny pinpricks forming a half-moon shape.

"I think the snake had a long, pointed tail," Sam said.

"He did," Amelia said. She used her other hand to wipe beads of perspiration from her top lip. "But he coiled and hissed before Crystal grabbed him."

The mere movement of her head shaking in disapproval made Amelia unsteady. Gram scooted closer to keep the girl from falling.

"You're probably just fine, but I'd feel better if we got you into Darton to the hospital, dear," Gram said.

Amelia snatched her arm away from Brynna, then winced.

"Definitely," Brynna agreed.

"But if I go to the hospital, they'll call my parents," Amelia moaned.

"We'll need to call them anyway," Brynna told her.

"And they'll make me come home—"

"Maybe not, Amelia," Gram said.

"—and I won't be able to ride Jinx in the race."

In the sudden quiet, Sam heard a siren approaching from the direction of Three Ponies Ranch. Jake's father, Luke Ely, was captain of the volunteer fire department, so it made sense he'd be first to respond.

Poor Dad. If he and the hands were close enough to home to hear it, he'd be worried all over again. First the sheriff's car and now the fire department. He'd never leave them home alone again.

Sam was feeling almost amused, when Amelia's words echoed in her mind.

I won't be able to ride Jinx in the race.

"The claiming race?" Sam asked. "What made you think *you* were going to ride Jinx?"

"Samantha," Gram tsked her tongue.

"Sorry. I didn't mean to sound rude, but—"

"Clara said I could," Amelia answered.

"What?" Sam yelped.

"When I called her yesterday," Amelia said, weakly.

Gram, Sam, and Brynna exchanged quick looks.

"So you weren't calling your parents yesterday," Brynna said.

"No," Amelia said. She swallowed hard. "Can I

have some water? I'm really thirsty."

"Shock," Gram said. "Poisonous snakebite or not, she's acting shocky." Gram bent to look into Amelia's eyes. "We'd better get her examined by a doctor."

Chapter Sixteen ❧

"Here comes the volunteer fire engine," Brynna said. "Luke's trained as a first responder, so let's get his opinion, too."

In minutes, the volunteer firefighters had checked out the snakebite and agreed with Brynna. Although the small wound was painful and a little swollen, they were virtually certain the snake hadn't injected any venom.

Just the same, Brynna and Gram loaded Amelia into the Buick for a trip to Darton County Hospital. They'd decided to leave Sam behind with Crystal.

"Sam, your dad should be home soon," Brynna said. "In the meantime, just make sure you feed the stock before dark and make yourselves something for dinner."

Brynna's lips hardened into a straight line as she studied Crystal, standing on the front porch beside Sam.

"While I'm in town, I'll take care of calling the girls' parents and notifying HARP."

Sam glared at Crystal. Even though the girl finally looked her age, hanging her head as if she hoped her dark hair would curtain her face from them, Sam didn't feel sorry for her.

"Placing blame isn't going to help at this point," Brynna said.

"Okay," Sam replied, but why shouldn't she yell at Crystal? She'd almost certainly cost them the HARP program.

And the ironic thing, Sam thought, was that Amelia had learned not to be a follower. She'd stood up to Crystal even though it put her in danger.

Car keys jingled as Brynna glanced into the Buick's back seat where Amelia sat with Gram, then waved good-bye.

As soon as the car crossed the bridge and rolled from sight, Sam opened the screen door. Its creak and slam were the only sounds. Sam didn't ask Crystal to follow her, but she did.

Inside, Blaze greeted Sam with a whine. She sank to her knees beside him, then circled his neck in a hug.

Now that the danger had passed, Sam's hands

trembled and her insides felt like shaking jello.

Blaze smelled dusty and doggy, but Sam pressed her face into his fur.

"It's okay, Blaze," she said. "Everything's okay now."

When she realized Crystal was looking down on her, Sam stood. She took a pitcher of iced tea from the refrigerator. Amber puddles of tea slopped onto the counter as she poured two full glasses. She added two spoonfuls of sugar to hers, then sat down. She leaned back in her chair, waiting for Crystal to make the next move.

Amazingly, Crystal took a paper towel from the roll and blotted up the spilled tea.

But so what? That could have been a rattlesnake. Instead of being checked "just in case," Amelia could be fighting for her life.

With the soggy paper towel still in her hand, Crystal started talking.

"I just want to go home. Why can't he let me stay home?" Crystal still faced the counter instead of Sam.

Would you want yourself around? Sam thought, but she didn't say it. Even angry as she was, that was too harsh.

"Think about what you've been doing," Sam said, instead.

"But I'm his daughter!" Crystal whirled, shouting. "He should love me no matter what!"

"Are you testing him?" Sam asked. "Trying to see

how much he'll take?"

"So what if I am?" Crystal's chin jerked upward and her eyes were defiant again.

"That's pretty mean," Sam said. "What do you think he'll say about today?"

"That I'm crazy. I mean, sometimes, I don't know. It's like I can't tell the difference between brave and crazy. I kinda think that if I could just stay home for a while, and be quiet, I could get that straight."

"Why don't you call your dad and tell him that?" Sam asked.

"Like he'll believe me after talking to Brynna," Crystal said.

"She's not in Darton yet. The drive takes a half hour. Call him now, Crystal. Get to him first so that he hears it from you."

Crystal's eyebrows rose. She looked tempted. Then she glanced at the clock.

"He's a dealer at the casino and he works the graveyard shift. He's probably getting ready for work."

"Fine," Sam said. She stood, then patted her jeans so Blaze would heel. "You sit here and think of excuses. Blaze and I are going to go feed the stock."

"You don't know what it's like," Crystal said. "He's always disappointed in me."

"Then do something right," Sam said and, before she started sounding even more like some lecturing adult, she walked out, slamming the door behind her.

* * *

As Sam checked the horses' water troughs, she scolded herself for trying to tell Crystal what to do. She was no expert, so why had she even tried?

As she shooed the hens inside for the night, Sam kicked herself for encouraging Crystal to stay on River Bend Ranch until the program ended on Friday. She didn't even like the girl, so why had she done that?

As she measured out grain and vitamin supplements for Dark Sunshine, she wondered what would be happening this time next week. The first week of HARP would be over. The claiming race would be over, too.

"Blaze!" Sam called as the border collie began sniffing around in the tack room. "Come back here."

Waving his tail, he waited as she filled her arms with flakes of hay for Popcorn and Jinx. The two mustangs nickered from the round pen, but Sam didn't hurry. She kept Blaze beside her and watched each rock, shrub, and shadow for snakes.

Crystal had been in the house for about half an hour when she called from the front porch.

"Sam! Phone."

Brushing away the hay prickling through her shirt, Sam hurried toward the house. Brynna had had time to get to Darton. It was probably her.

Feeling overheated after working outside, Sam slid open a kitchen window before taking the telephone from Crystal. As she did, she noticed Crystal wore a lopsided smile.

Oh my gosh, what's up now? Sam wondered, but she'd stalled long enough.

"Hello?"

The caller turned out to be Clara.

"Linc Slocum just stopped in for pie and coffee—" Clara broke off and Sam could hear Linc Slocum's voice in the background. She pictured the telephone next to the coffee shop cash register and imagined Linc standing there, instructing Clara what to say. "He mentioned he passed Brynna and Grace on the road."

"They were heading for town like a coyote for a campground," Linc's voice boomed.

Sam joined in as Clara laughed.

Linc Slocum was the richest man in this part of Nevada, but more than anything, he wanted people to think of him as a cowboy. He was greedy, gossipy, and prone to buying anything that might give him Western credentials. One of those things was the Phantom.

Linc Slocum didn't care if he owned the Phantom through legal or illegal means. He'd scarred the stallion by snubbing him to barrels filled with concrete. He'd tried to adopt him through the BLM and failed. He'd arranged for the wild stallion to be taken off the range by a shady rodeo promoter who'd drugged and abused him. Linc Slocum never stopped trying to take away the Phantom's freedom, and Sam despised him for it.

But since Clara was calling and Linc was just waiting in the background, it might be okay to explain why Gram and Brynna had been driving so fast toward town.

"We, uh, had an accident out here. Amelia's fine, but she was bitten by a snake. Gram and Brynna just took her into town to be checked out by a doctor."

As Clara sympathized, Sam watched Crystal.

The dark-haired girl blushed, but she also fidgeted with what looked like excitement.

Meeting Sam's eyes, Crystal mouthed silent words that looked like, *I have to tell you something.*

" — can you?" Clara asked, dragging Sam's attention back to their phone conversation.

"I'm sorry, Clara, what were you asking me?"

"I don't blame you for being surprised, Sam. It is short notice, but I've already paid the entry fee and there are already bids on the horse and he has to be ridden by someone under sixteen."

Sam heard Linc's voice bellowing questions, but she asked anyway.

"Clara? Are you saying you want me to ride Jinx in the claiming race? I've never — "

Clara chuckled. "It's more for fun than an actual race," she said. "I never would have agreed to let that Amelia do it if I thought it was risky. Although" — Clara broke off to tsk her tongue — "that girl promised to get me written permission from her parents, and I haven't seen it yet."

"But it's not a real race?" Sam prodded her.

"There's a running start, like a barrel race, and only one horse runs at a time," Clara explained. "The clock starts ticking when you cross a line into that little arena the YRA uses. When you reach the other end of the arena, you swing a turn, then race back. Time stops when you cross over that line again."

"Like a barrel race with no barrels," Sam mused.

"Yes, ma'am," Clara agreed. "So, what do you think?"

Sam pictured Jinx balking and the crowd roaring with laughter.

Jinx could embarrass them both. Still, if he did balk, he'd probably do it outside the arena, before they got started.

"It's mainly for fun," Clara coaxed. "The entry fee was seventy-five dollars, and the purse is five hundred."

"I don't know," Sam hesitated. "He's really fast, but he balks, Clara. And he's still a little unpredictable."

"Oh honey, that doesn't make any difference. Maybe you didn't hear me before. There are already three bids on the horse. The minimum bid is the same as the purse—five hundred dollars!"

Three bids. So Jinx would have a new home, no matter how he ran in the claiming race. Who could have placed those bids?

"I'll have to ask my dad," Sam said, but she already felt the anticipation building.

Dad had to say yes.

"You do that, Sam," Clara said, raising her voice over Linc's chatter. "And I'll pay you a rider's fee, of course." Clara paused to listen and Sam wondered why Linc hadn't just picked up the phone and called River Bend Ranch himself.

"Oh, is that so?" Clara sounded pleased.

"What, Clara?"

All at once, worry grabbed Sam.

"Linc was just telling me—how much?"

Sam gripped the receiver harder.

"Linc was just saying," Clara continued, "that he can always use another fast horse. He's planning on watching the race Saturday and thinks it would add to the fun to have a stake in it."

"What's he mean by that?" Sam asked, though she knew very well what Linc Slocum meant.

"Well, it sounds to me like he wants to make a claiming bid on my horse."

"Darn right!" Linc's voice roared.

Sam closed her eyes. Jinx would go to the highest bidder.

In all of Darton County, there was only one millionaire. If Linc Slocum bid on Jinx, the grulla gelding would be his.

Chapter Seventeen ❧

𝒲orking like a robot, Sam took a package of hot dogs from the freezer and tried to make dinner. Three hot dogs exploded in the microwave before she got the knack of cooking them. Sam served the first two survivors to Crystal, though Blaze stood by, wagging his tail hopefully.

The dark-haired girl stayed silent while they ate, and Sam appreciated that, but when she'd blotted up the last drip of mustard with her hot dog bun, she still hadn't figured out how to help Jinx.

"I have to tell you what my dad said," Crystal said, finally breaking the silence.

"Okay," Sam said. She stared at the kitchen window, which only showed her reflection against the dark-gray night outside. She wondered what her own father was doing now.

"I told him about the snake and then I told him I was going to beg Brynna to let me stay and finish the HARP course—"

"If there is one," Sam said.

"—and he said he'd call HARP and tell them what progress I was making, and if she'd let me and I stuck it out and didn't mess up anymore, he'd come watch on Friday."

While Crystal waited for Sam to celebrate, crunching filled the kitchen. Blaze was eating his dinner, but he, too, watched Sam with reproachful looks. Probably, she thought, because the smell of hot dogs still lingered.

Sam just couldn't work up the enthusiasm Crystal wanted from her.

"So, he's not going to punish you?" she asked.

"I'm grounded for the summer. I can't go anywhere without him." Crystal frowned, tapped her glass, then added, "How sick is it that I like the sound of that?"

Sam shrugged.

"Do you know what he said about sending me away? He thinks he's been doing a terrible job as a father because of the wild stuff I've done. He even said because he rides a motorcycle instead of driving a car, he had to send me away so I could be exposed to people who'd have a better influence on me."

Before Sam had a chance to respond, Blaze jumped up from his dish and paced to the door.

Tires bumped over the bridge just an instant before hoofbeats.

Amelia and Gram came into the kitchen while Dad and Brynna lingered outside.

"They're bedding down the horses," Gram explained, but Sam knew better. Brynna was telling Dad everything that had happened in his absence, and Dad was probably frustrated because he hadn't been home to help.

Amelia held up a bandaged right hand.

"We were right," she said. "It wasn't a rattle-snake."

"Does it hurt?" Crystal asked.

"Yeah, but that's not why it's all wrapped up." Amelia gave an impish smile. "They were going to just put a Band-Aid on it until I convinced everyone I could still ride. So they added lots of extra protection."

"Are you sure?" Sam asked.

Amelia made a loose fist with her left hand and held it out to one side as if she were holding reins.

"Brynna said I could."

Sam glanced over at Gram.

"We thought—and her parents agreed—that Amelia's progress in other areas should be rewarded."

Amelia pumped her bandaged hand skyward as she smiled at Sam.

"Good job," Sam said.

"But she is *not* riding in the claiming race," Gram insisted.

Amelia's eyes slid away from Sam's and her grin faded. Sam rubbed her eyes. She was tired, but she could swear Amelia's expression showed more guilt than disappointment.

The kitchen door opened. Brynna and Dad walked in and Sam looked quickly enough to see them loosen hands, which must have been linked while they were outside.

Although seeing Dad holding hands with Brynna had taken some getting used to, Sam knew now that it was a good sign.

Just the same, his eyes took in everyone in the kitchen critically, then remained on Crystal.

The dark-haired girl seemed to think Dad was asking for a confession.

"I'm the one who—"

Dad held his hand palm out, halting her.

"Young lady, I've been in the saddle about forty hours these last two days. I've heard what I need to hear from my wife. The rest can wait. Just now, I'm gonna have a shower, then come down to eat whatever I smell cooking."

"Just hot dogs, Dad," Sam told him. "And half of them exploded."

Gram's head was tilted to one side as she peered inside the microwave oven, surveying the mess. Dad didn't notice.

The hand he rested on Sam's shoulder smelled of horses and leather.

"Sounds like a fine dinner to me," he said. "And I hear you did a good job today during the—emergency."

Dad's eyes looked weary in his sun-browned face, but mostly he looked proud.

"I didn't really do anything," Sam admitted. "And if I hadn't left to see Tempest—"

"You had permission," Brynna interrupted. "And by keeping calm, you kept Amelia quiet."

"Thanks," Sam sighed.

"You have the night off," Brynna said.

"Right," Sam laughed. "After I clean out the microwave I trashed." But Brynna looked serious, so Sam asked, "What do you mean?"

"She means I'll be sleeping in the bunkhouse tonight with the girls," Gram said.

Sam pictured herself falling backward in slow motion onto her own bed. Just the idea made her relax. Her head bobbed on her neck. Her shoulders drooped and she could barely see past her heavy eyelids.

"Thanks, Gram," Sam said.

Dad winked as he passed through the swinging door to the living room.

When his boots sounded on the stairs, Amelia whispered to Sam, "I need to talk to you."

She sat back in surprise as all eyes turned her way.

"A whisper attracts a lot more attention than a shout around here," Brynna said.

"I guess so," Amelia muttered. "But Sam, we have to talk about the race."

"Amelia won't be riding in it." Brynna sounded as if her patience had been tested on the subject. "Even without the injury, she wouldn't have."

Sam decided this wasn't the time to mention the pending permission slip Clara had told her about.

"But I have to tell you something," Amelia insisted.

Crystal shifted as if trying to draw Amelia's attention, but the other girl just stared at Sam.

The way she was bugging her eyes, it must be important, but Brynna thought otherwise.

"Amelia, is it anything that's going to change before tomorrow morning?"

After a thoughtful minute, Amelia shook her head.

"Now," Brynna said to Sam, "if you're going to be alert for our five thirty meeting, I think you should hustle upstairs and get some rest."

Sam groaned at the thought of the early meeting. If they were staying on schedule, though, it must mean Brynna's talks with the girls' parents and HARP had gone well.

Tomorrow the girls would mount up for the first time.

Amelia would be ecstatic. Crystal would be scared. Both reactions would take extra attention from Brynna and Sam.

When she got upstairs, Sam wondered if her bedside clock had stopped. Could it be only eight o'clock?

It was. Her watch confirmed it. It was way too early to go to bed. Yawning, she picked up a horse magazine she'd barely read, and flopped down on her quilt.

After a minute or two, she realized she wasn't really reading the article on barn buckets. Her mind was replaying Gram's story about luck.

The cowboy who'd owned Jinx said he was a bad luck charm, but Sam thought he was wrong.

Jinx had been sold by the Potters because Mr. Potter had broken his arm in a fall from the grulla, but then the Happy Heart Ranch had been sold for a huge amount of money.

When the cowboy had traded Jinx to Clara for a dollar and a piece of cake, she'd counted herself lucky, until Jinx escaped and caused Jake's accident.

But maybe, because he needed the money to pay for his car insurance, Jake would agree to work for the HARP program. So, the luck seesawed back to good, at least for the girls who'd benefit from his teaching, didn't it?

Sam stared at her bedroom's plastered ceiling. Letting her gaze lose focus, she could see pictures in the white, uneven surface.

Jinx and the Phantom had run side by side,

revealing the grulla's hidden talent for speed. That speed had caused Amelia to dream of riding him. Having a dream reminded her she needed to be a good kid to get her parents' cooperation to ride again. Maybe that realization had helped her stand up to Crystal.

And Jinx's speed had inspired Clara to enter him in the claiming race, so she might earn some extra money and the gelding could go to a home where they didn't consider him bad luck.

Sam closed her eyes. She sighed, then fell asleep knowing they'd all live happily ever after.

Only in her dreams did Sam feel a threat. Looming dark in the corner of her mind, she saw Linc Slocum, ready to tilt Jinx's luck back the other way.

Chapter Eighteen ❧

Before breakfast, Sam talked with Brynna and Dad about riding in the claiming race.

Dad took a deep breath and glanced at Brynna. Sam followed his eyes in time to notice Brynna's arched eyebrows.

"How 'bout you go help the girls groom and saddle their horses right now," Dad said, "and we'll let you know."

She'd gone without a word, but now breakfast was over, the horses were ready for Amelia and Crystal to mount up for the first time, and still Sam hadn't heard a word about the claiming race.

Patience, she told herself, and turned back to work.

"Amelia, I noticed you frowned every time you had to pick up your spoon for a bite of oatmeal," Sam pointed out as they left the kitchen. "How's your hand?"

"It doesn't hurt," Amelia insisted, flexing her fingers in demonstration. "I just don't like oatmeal."

Sam smiled and glanced over her shoulder at Crystal.

"Slowpoke," she said, and though Crystal stuck out her tongue, Sam knew it was really fear that slowed Crystal's steps.

Or maybe it was more than that, Sam thought as Amelia walked ahead. She hadn't heard Amelia speak a single word to Crystal since yesterday when she'd screamed at her to put the snake down.

Crystal's feelings had to be hurt, but what did she expect?

Sam shook her head. She hoped the girls worked it out, but her job was to get them in their saddles and into the round pen before Brynna finished her last cup of coffee.

"Who wants to go first?" Sam asked when the horses were tacked up.

"Me, me, me!" Amelia insisted.

"Okay, now I'm going to let you try it your own way, but make sure Jinx doesn't move off once you have your boot in the stirrup."

"Okay," Amelia said impatiently.

"You remember how he did that with me?" Sam

said, touching Amelia's left hand as she gathered her reins to mount. "Think a minute."

"I remember," Amelia insisted. "He won't do that with me. We're buddies."

Sure enough, Jinx let Amelia mount without a fuss. Had he become more confident after days of kind handling, or was there really a bond between the two?

"I wouldn't do this except for my dad," Crystal said, tightening her ponytail. "Everybody told me I was lucky I didn't kill myself when I jumped off the school roof into the swimming pool—"

Amelia's head whipped around to stare at Crystal. Apparently she hadn't heard about that misdeed. Still, Amelia didn't speak to the other girl.

"—but the pool was just sitting there," Crystal went on. "It wasn't trying to kill me. I'm not so sure about him."

Popcorn's ears pricked toward Jinx, wondering where they were going, but he waited quietly for Crystal to mount up and decide.

"Popcorn wouldn't think of killing you," Sam said.

The screen door creaked open as Brynna came outside. She walked toward the round pen, smiling at Sam's last words.

As Sam watched, Brynna gave her a thumbs-up sign. That must mean she'd get to ride Jinx in the claiming race.

Oh my gosh. It was only a few days away. How could she train a horse who was afraid to gallop to burst into a run practically from a standing start?

"If he decides he doesn't like me he will," Crystal said.

"Will what?" Sam asked.

"Kill me!" Crystal snapped. "Haven't you been listening? Look at him. He has the coldest eyes."

Sam didn't point out that Crystal's and Popcorn's eyes were a perfect match.

"He likes you," she insisted.

As Amelia reined Popcorn toward the gate Brynna held open, the girl muttered something.

It sounded like, *That's because he doesn't know her.*

Inch by inch, Crystal mounted the albino gelding.

"You look great up there," Sam said, and it was true.

The albino's white coat sparkled from good grooming. Crystal's royal-blue tee-shirt brought out Popcorn's blue eyes as well as her own. And the horse seemed set on pleasing Crystal. Although her rein movements were clumsy and should have been confusing, he followed Jinx into the round pen and did as he was asked all morning.

Finally, they released the horses just before lunch.

"Why do you like riding so much?" Brynna asked Amelia as they walked back to the house.

"It's because," Amelia looked down as if she was afraid of their response, "they have minds. It's not like riding a bike where it just does what you make it do. If a horse goes along with what you're asking, it's because he wants to. That's what makes it fun."

"That's what makes it dangerous," Crystal grumbled.

At last, Amelia broke her silence toward Crystal.

"I don't know how you can think that," Amelia said. "I mean, Sam was riding this close"—Amelia measured off a few inches of air between her thumb and forefinger—"to a wild stallion and she didn't get hurt."

"Wait a minute!" Brynna said.

"Yeah, wait," Sam said. "Don't even think of doing that, you guys, ever."

"Don't worry 'bout me," Crystal muttered, but Amelia crossed her arms, looking more rebellious than she had all week.

"I'm lucky because the Phantom is my friend," Sam said, trying to explain. "But it's because I raised him from a foal. Not because wild horses like people."

"You bonded with him like I did with Jinx," Amelia insisted.

"Not exactly. Jinx hasn't been wild for a long time. The Phantom is a mustang first, the leader of his herd. Our friendship is way down the list of who he is."

Brynna nodded, apparently pleased with Sam's explanation, but Amelia was still skeptical and Crystal was surprised.

"You don't sound that sad about it," Crystal said.

Sam sighed. There was no point in talking about the number of times the stallion had bruised her heart by ignoring her, or acting like the wild thing he was.

"If he acted like a pet," Sam said, "he couldn't protect his mares and foals. Whenever he's trusted humans, they've tried to take away his freedom."

As Gram leaned from the door and told them to hurry and wash up or their fruit salads would be too warm to eat, Amelia grabbed Sam's sleeve.

"What I have to tell you can't wait anymore."

"Oh, I forgot," Sam said. "Sorry."

"I used my parents' credit card to make a bid on Jinx."

"What?" Sam's mind spun. She must be talking about the claiming race, but Amelia hadn't left the ranch except to go to the emergency room yesterday.

"On my cell phone, the day I found the flier about the race. It had all the rules and registration information and a direct number to that YRA organization. So I, uh, put a bid on Jinx. What am I going to do?"

"Right now," Sam said, "you're going to be thankful I can't think hard and strangle you at the same time."

After lunch, Brynna watched the girls take turns riding Popcorn in the round pen while Dad helped Sam work with Jinx.

"If I don't like the way things go, I reserve the

right to change my mind," he told Sam, but after watching the horse make three quarter-mile sprints with Sam aboard, he shook his head.

"Don't see the problem. Whatever was wrong with him, you seem to have—" Dad stopped. "That sounds a mite too optimistic, doesn't it?"

Sam laughed. "No, I think he's a good horse."

"Good and smart are two different things."

"Dad!" Sam said. Even though she should be used to it by now, she hated it when Dad treated horses like animals.

"Whatever made him balk that way is still in his narrow cayuse head," Dad said, rubbing the grulla's face with affection. "He can't know it's over with. Anything could stir it up all over again."

"Shall we keep doing this until he balks?" Sam asked.

"No point in it," Dad said. "When something triggers that fear, he'll stop. Until then, all you can do is be real nice to this fella, so maybe he'll forget."

Sam returned to help Brynna instruct the girls, just as they took a lemonade break.

"So what do you think?" Amelia said under her breath as Brynna talked with Crystal about her promise to her father.

"You don't have a pasture for Jinx, do you?" Sam asked. "At your house in New Mexico?"

"Rub it in," Amelia's tone was mean. "Just because

you have acres and acres of pasture and range."

Sam waited until Amelia stopped, then said, "I didn't have a horse when I lived in San Francisco. I know it's frustrating."

"I have a yard. It's not real big, but it's fenced," Amelia said.

"Would Jinx be happy there?" Sam asked.

Amelia glared at Sam. Then she turned to Jinx and rubbed her hands over the gelding's smooth neck.

"Of course he wouldn't," she admitted. "And now, while my parents are actually thinking I might turn back into an okay kid—I mean, they might even let me take riding lessons again—it's a dumb time to charge a thousand dollars on their credit card."

"A thousand dollars!" Sam hissed, hoping Brynna wouldn't hear. "The minimum bid is just five hundred."

"I wanted to make sure I had the highest bid," Amelia admitted.

Sam's breath caught in her throat. If Amelia's bid stood, maybe Linc Slocum's offer wouldn't be the highest. Then he couldn't claim Jinx. But what Amelia had done was against the law.

Good luck. Bad luck. Did the seesawing never stop?

"You've got to do what you think is best," Sam managed to say, but she didn't think her own words would come back to haunt her so soon.

❊ ❊ ❊

Sam was alone in the house when the telephone rang.

Dad, Brynna, and Gram had taken the girls on a late night hike up to the top of the ridge to look at constellations.

Although Crystal complained that it was a lame and nerdy thing to do, Sam could tell she was excited about walking through the wilds by starlight.

"Snakes aren't out at this time of night, right?" Amelia asked with a slight tremble in her voice.

"Almost never," Brynna said.

And that was when Crystal gave Amelia a hug, and when Sam decided to stay behind. She hoped the two girls would become friendly equals if she just stayed home.

"Hello?" Sam said into the phone.

"Hello, ma'am?" said an unfamiliar voice with a southern accent. "My name is Henry Fox and I'm calling to speak to a Samantha Forester."

Even though the man had mispronounced her last name, his name was vaguely familiar and the call couldn't be for anyone else.

"I'm Samantha Forster," she said.

"Oh."

Sam listened hard. Long-distance static whirred on the telephone line, but the man stayed quiet.

"Mr. Fox?" she asked.

"See, the thing is, I called to see how H. B. was

doing. Silly, for an old hand like me to get attached, but I did. When I called the cafe, a waitress named Millie said the gal I wanted to talk with was Clara. And seems like Clara's not working tonight."

"Who's H. B.?" Sam asked, but the man didn't seem to hear.

"Well, this Millie said I should talk with you, seein' as it's about the horse, but, begging your pardon, ma'am, you sound like a kid."

"I'm fourteen," Sam said, but she wasn't offended. Her mind suddenly brightened with memory.

Henry Fox was the cowboy who'd traded Jinx to Clara for a dollar and a piece of cake. He'd called to see how the horse was doing. Did that mean he wanted the grulla back?

"Are you talking about Jinx? The grulla gelding?"

"Yes ma'am, I am," he said in a wondering tone. "But don't tell me you're the one's been riding him."

"Sure I have," Sam said proudly.

"I never thought she'd use him with kids." The man's voice was so low, he might have been talking to himself. "Seemed like a shrewd old girl. Clara, that is. Jinx was just a joke name, but I never meant for H. B. to . . ." He cleared his throat. "Has anyone been hurt?"

For a second, Sam wondered if he'd heard about Amelia's snakebite. Then she realized he was still talking about Jinx.

"No," Sam said slowly. "Are you worried because of the way he balks?"

"That's just it," he said in a despairing tone. "After the balking comes the bucking and, well, shoot, there's no reason not to come clean with you, I guess. Here's the thing. H. B.—Heart Breaker, he was called—"

"Because of his brand," Sam supplied.

"Yes, ma'am. H. B. was broke to be a bareback bronc—"

Sam gasped. She thought of the color, clamor, and crowds at rodeos. Jinx couldn't be a rodeo bronc.

"—didn't do good at it, 'cause he was always wanting to run," the man continued.

"He loves to run," Sam agreed.

"Makes me feel real downhearted when you say it that way, because he did used to love it. But see, a rodeo rider gets no points if he comes out of the chute and the bronc just runs with him. The bronc is supposed to buck. And, well, that's why I had to take H. B. before they put him down.

"They were just amateurs, the kids who bought him from Potter to use in rodeo. Seems like even though they whipped and spurred him, trying to push him through the gallop and straight into his buck, it didn't work.

"He gave up, though, in a way. Once you got on him, he just wouldn't move at all."

"That's awful," Sam said. "But I think he's doing fine, now."

Sam gave the kitchen a quick glance and listened at the open window for the sound of feet or voices.

She didn't want anyone to have heard even her half of this conversation.

"And by fine, you mean . . . ?"

"He walks, jogs, lopes, even gallops," Sam said.

The cowboy's sigh was so gusty and loud, Sam could practically feel the phone shudder.

"All right, then," he said. "All right. That's good."

Still, he seemed reluctant to hang up.

"I'm guessing that if you keep him away from arenas and places that bring back thoughts of the bad old days, he'll be just fine. Good evenin' ma'am, and good luck."

Chapter Nineteen ⟡

Do what you think is right.

On the morning of the claiming race Sam was still trying to figure out what she thought was right.

Cross-tied in a stall at the Darton County fairgrounds, Jinx's coat shone with a hue that made passersby stop and stare.

It seemed everyone had a different name for the coat color—steeldust, lilac dun, blue slate, silver buckskin.

Even Clara tried to come up with a perfect description.

"Looks like you took gold nuggets and lumps of sterling silver, whirled them up in a blender, and poured them all over him," she said.

"Don't believe anyone but a cook would think of that," Dad said to Clara. "But this gelding *is* looking mighty fine."

"While you were off checking in, some folks who came by were disappointed that bidding closed twenty-four hours before race time," Clara said.

"It did?" Sam asked.

"Yep, a lot of people see this as a nice chance to help YRA and get a real bargain, too," Clara said.

From talk around the fairgrounds, Sam knew most people had come to watch their children compete in YRA-sponsored games on horseback. Still, some were hoping to claim one of the eight horses running, for a bargain price.

Sam watched Jinx's ears.

Since the fairgrounds box stall was complimentary overnight with the entry fee, she and Dad had driven the truck and horse trailer down to Darton yesterday.

Though he didn't admit it, she knew Dad had been happy to escape socializing with Amelia's and Crystal's parents. He'd been polite, shaking their hands after they'd arrived, but then he'd turned shy and silent. Sam was sorry to miss the girls' rides on Popcorn. Still, after she'd talked with Henry Fox, it had been more important to see Jinx's reaction to the arena before the race.

"What's Jinx think of it here?" Clara asked.

"I rode him around the arena and he was fine,"

Sam said. "The worst thing he's done is sidestep when he saw a bright yellow candy wrapper."

"Fifteen minutes 'til race time," Dad said, glancing at Sam's watch. "Wonder where Brynna and those folks are."

"Sam!"

All of a sudden, she saw Amelia run a zigzag pattern through the gathering crowd. Jinx threw his head up in surprise, but didn't act scared.

So far, so good, Sam thought, as Amelia grabbed her sleeve and tugged her down to whisper in her ear.

"I got through on my cell phone yesterday just before the deadline for bids closed," she said.

"Yeah?"

"And I withdrew my bid."

Dizziness spun Sam's head, though she stood still. She wouldn't have to worry about an inexperienced rider like Amelia ending up with an ex-bucking horse. Without Amelia's thousand-dollar bid, though, who would claim Jinx?

"My parents were so impressed with the way I rode yesterday that I get to take riding lessons again. Gotta go," she said. "Everyone else is waiting. Bye."

Amelia scampered back to the others and Sam waved. Amelia's parents were small people, not much taller than their daughter, and though they looked as if they felt out of place at the YRA fun day, they also looked proud.

Crystal stood with a big man who wore a leather vest over a tee-shirt and jeans. Sam would bet he outweighed Dad two-to-one. Though his eyes were hidden by mirrored sunglasses, Sam thought Crystal's father looked proud, too.

Crystal gave Sam a small wave. She was smiling and Sam had a feeling everything would work out for both girls.

She wasn't so sure about herself.

"We'll be goin'," Dad said. "Tack up alone and have a little talk with that horse. Tell him not to do anything crazy."

By the time Sam said, "I will," Dad and Clara had already gone.

Almost holding her breath, Sam smoothed on a saddle blanket, then settled her saddle into place.

She'd only thought a minute before turning down Ryan Slocum's offer of a lightweight racing saddle. She was more at home riding in a Western saddle, and every bit of balance would count if Jinx reverted to his bucking horse training.

A few minutes later, Sam walked to the end of her reins and looked back at the gelding. All his tack was in place and he shone like tarnished silver.

As if he could tell her mind had wandered, Jinx strode forward and Sam stood beside him.

"You're going to be a good boy for me, aren't you, Jinx?" Sam asked, tracing her finger over the grulla's broken heart brand. "I've never hurt you, and I promise, if the person who claims you ever does, I'll take you back."

For the first time since that moment on the range, the big horse swung his head around and pressed his forehead to Sam's.

"I promise," she told him, and Jinx answered with a snort.

When the claiming race finally began, Sam felt strangely detached from the action. If Jinx bucked her off and she was injured, she'd have no one to blame but herself. She should be afraid, but she wasn't.

A gray pony named Starlight ran first, and finished the quarter-mile sprint to great applause.

"Claimed by Toni and Tara Franklin," the announcer said, and two little girls met the pony with hugs just past the finish line.

"Tiger Prince," the announcer boomed over the microphone as a long-legged horse with marbled orange-and-black markings stepped up to the starting line, then reared and threw his rider.

"I guess the Tiger Prince has a little more gumption than his rider figured."

When the crowd laughed, the announcer went on making jokes at the rider's expense.

Sam felt sick. That could be her.

At last the rider, a teenage boy, caught the horse, remounted, and rode him at a fast trot across the arena and back.

Nightingale, a black horse with white stockings on both hind legs, made the best time of the day, and was claimed by a representative from Sterling Stables.

Then it was Jinx's turn.

"Come to find out," the announcer drawled, "this horse was sold to Clara from down at the Alkali coffee shop for one dollar bill and a slice of the best pineapple upside-down cake in the world."

The area just outside the arena was cleared for a running start. To Sam, the crowd's laughter sounded faint and far away. Only Jinx seemed real.

Sam leaned forward and whispered to him.

"This is your chance to show them who you really are, boy. Not Potter's spooky cow pony, not a failed bucking bronc, not a bad luck charm."

She was about to give Jinx the signal to go, when he shied.

Sam swayed in the saddle, fighting the urge to grab the saddle horn as she looked all around.

A boy had dropped a bag of popcorn. That couldn't be it. Pigtailed twins were tugging each of their mother's hands. That wouldn't frighten Jinx, either.

With a snort, Jinx lifted his front hooves from the dirt and swung his head from side to side.

Tiger Prince and his rider stood yards across the fairground. No one had come forward to claim the horse. His rider was shouting at him and brandishing a riding whip.

The whip.

Jinx squealed and clacked his teeth.

Dallas had told her that even when Jinx was a yearling, he hated the whip.

Henry Fox had said they punished the bolting H. B. with a whip.

Dad had told her he thought Jinx would be fine—unless something triggered a fearful memory.

Tension made each of the grulla's legs straighten and plant. He wasn't going anywhere.

Sam leaned her cheek against the gelding's hot neck and stroked it with all the tenderness her fingers held.

"You're fine, boy," she whispered. "Kindness cured all that. You don't have to remember."

"When you're ready," boomed the announcer.

"You're a good horse Jinx," Sam made one last try to convince him. "Let's show 'em all!"

Sam clapped her heels against him and Jinx was off.

As if he'd raced every day of his life, he bounded from a standstill to a run.

Sam moved forward. After three strides, Jinx's gait was smooth, effortless, the ground-eating gallop of a mustang running the range for the sheer joy of feeling his muscles lengthen and bunch.

They reached the far end of the arena and swung a turn so quick it tore tears from Sam's eyes. Then they were stampeding back and the finish line was coming up way too fast. Sam shifted in the saddle.

She couldn't wave away the people rushing forward to catch Jinx, for fear he'd catch the movement from the corner of one eye and stumble. So she let him run. Seeing his speed, the people scattered.

Sam closed her fingers on the reins, gradually pulling them in. Jinx slowed, still prancing as if he had energy to spare.

Chin tucked, ears pricked forward, the grulla lifted his knees and arched his neck. Was he dancing in joy? Sam crossed her fingers and hoped the horse had a reason to celebrate.

Just ahead, people lined both sides of the path back to the arena. Sam saw Dad, Brynna, and Gram. Crystal was bouncing up and down and Amelia was pulling on her mother's sleeve, pointing at Jinx and chattering.

Sam saw lots of strangers, too. What if one of them stepped forward to claim Jinx? Sam settled forward against the gelding's neck, knowing this hug might be their last.

Please let the right person win Jinx!

Sam could hear the announcer's voice but not what he was saying. When Linc Slocum, huffing and red-faced, elbowed through the clapping crowd to block the path before her, Sam's spirits sank.

Please, not him.

"I've been robbed, and don't tell me you had nothing to do with this, Samantha Forster!" Linc yelled.

Sam wanted to shout for joy. If Linc was unhappy,

everything was all right.

Jinx's ears flattened. Sam gathered her reins, but the gelding still bolted forward, narrowly missing Slocum's shoulder.

"How was I supposed to know the deadline for bidding ended yesterday morning? How?" Linc roared. "Tell me that?"

"You could have read the rules like everyone else!" a small voice soared above the noisy crowd.

"Who said that!" Linc turned on his heel, but not quickly enough to see Amelia yanked back a step by her mother.

"Jinx!" Sam gasped.

As Slocum turned away, the gelding bared his teeth and would have grabbed the man's shoulder if Sam hadn't sat hard and backed the horse away.

"Get that animal under control or I'm calling the cops!" Slocum threatened.

"Already here, Linc," Sheriff Ballard said.

Sam relaxed and she felt Jinx do the same.

The horse stopped pulling against the reins. He tossed his head one final time at Linc Slocum, then shook like a big dog.

"By rights," Slocum said in a lecturing tone, "this animal should be mine. I was unfairly excluded from entering a bid and I want you to look into it."

Sheriff Ballard probably sounded regretful to anyone who couldn't see his face, but Sam could. Under his sandy mustache, the sheriff grinned.

"I'm sorry, Linc, but I'm afraid that would be a conflict of interest."

"What? You're refusing—?"

Jinx's ears flattened once more. His hindquarters shifted and his tail lashed angrily.

"Linc, I'll thank you to step back from my horse," Sheriff Ballard said.

Grinning, Sam dismounted and handed Sheriff Ballard the reins.

Jinx looked between her and Sheriff Ballard, but the gelding didn't protest when the sheriff rubbed the broken heart brand on his shoulder.

"Congratulations," Sam said, and she meant it.

"I'm feeling pretty lucky for a man who just won a horse named Jinx," he said. "And I want to thank you, Samantha. Looks like you took care of mending this horse inside and out."

Sam took a few steps back from Jinx and his new owner, and stifled a sigh just before she noticed something she'd never seen before.

If she squinted her eyes just the right way while looking at Jinx, the dark markings on his shoulders looked like a wreath of winner's roses.

By the time Sam and Dad started back to River Bend Ranch, dusk had colored the range many shades of blue.

Driving the Buick, Brynna and Gram had quickly outdistanced Dad's truck. Just the same, Sam's eyes searched the blue-gray ribbon of highway unrolling ahead.

Blue-black mountains jutted up on the edge of the *playa*, like plates on a dinosaur's back. Sometime there might have been dinosaurs here. Their ancient bones must lie under the desert's crust along with those of Jake's Native American ancestors and the Phantom's forebears.

Where are you? Sam wondered, sending her thoughts to the stallion who'd once been hers.

He must be out there. A wild white stallion had roamed this range for as long as anyone could remember, and he'd challenged Jinx just days ago.

As her eyes scanned the spaces between boulders and bushes, searching for the stallion, Sam remembered him running shoulder to shoulder with Jinx.

Each time the grulla had lengthened his strides, the Phantom had drawn ahead.

On a racetrack or in an arena, Jinx might have beaten the Phantom, but it couldn't happen on the open range.

Sam's eyes burned with searching. She rubbed them.

"Tired out?" Dad asked. With a smile, he glanced away from the road.

"A little," Sam admitted. She sighed in weariness and told herself she wasn't going to see the Phantom tonight. She should quit fighting to stay awake.

Then, just as her eyelids drooped, she saw him.

She'd been staring far off, and he was close, only yards off the freeway, loping alone through the juniper bushes.

"Dad, stop!" Sam shouted.

No one who'd seen a wild, rough-coated mustang by day would believe a bone and blood stallion could seem a creature spun of moonbeams.

He was right there and he was amazing. She couldn't believe Dad was still driving. If he stopped, she just knew the Phantom would, too. How could he not want to see the stallion up close?

"Sam?" Dad's voice might have been miles away instead of right beside her in the truck.

Sam tried to answer, but she was hypnotized by the stallion. He seemed to skim above the dirt, shoulders glowing like pearls.

"Samantha!" Dad said.

Finally he'd stopped the truck, but he'd missed his chance.

The skidding tires startled the stallion. He shied and leaped down the bank of earth edging the highway.

Only when Dad's hand jostled her shoulder did Sam answer.

"Did you see him?" she whispered.

"See who?" Dad asked.

"The Phantom," she said, and then she pushed open the truck door and stood listening.

Far away, the La Charla river rushed, but somewhere closer, rocks rattled against one another, falling away from the Phantom's hooves.

"I hear something," Dad said. "But you need to get back inside, honey."

A summer breeze blew Sam's hair into her eyes. She held it back with both hands, scanning the range once more, and this time it was worth it.

For just an instant more, she saw the Phantom.

Like a faint frost outline of a horse, he was there — and then he was gone.

Sighing, Sam got back into the truck. She closed the door, then settled back into the seat with a smile.

"I think you were about half dreamin'," Dad said, as he began driving once more.

Sam took a deep breath, held it, then released it with a smile.

"Maybe," Sam said, because Dad was right. For her, the Phantom stallion was a dream come true.

From
Phantom Stallion
∽ 14 ∾
MOONRISE

Chapter Three∾

"It's just wind in the canyon. Now that the trees have leafed out, the acoustics are different." Jen's voice deepened as she stressed a logical explanation

"You're probably right," Sam said, though Ace's ears pricked forward with interest. With a wave, she aimed Ace toward home.

The sun shone from directly overhead. Ace seemed to jog within his own shadow. If he'd sensed that howl from the hills was worth fearing, he'd forgotten about it.

Sam was nearly home when she saw Dad. From his lazy wave, it was clear he'd spotted her first.

She'd come to expect that.

A lifelong cowboy, Dad could scan the brown and green vastness of the range and tell faraway rocks and bushes from cattle, deer, or mustangs. It sounded easy, but it wasn't. Sam couldn't count the number of times her heart had leaped up from spotting a wild horse, only to have it turn into a stunted pinion pine, dancing in the wind, when she got closer.

Dad swayed easily in the saddle as Jeepers-Creepers, his flea-bitten Appaloosa cow horse, descended a trail from the foothills.

Jeep seemed nervous. The rangy gray-and-white horse switched his rattail and looked behind him as if he feared he was being followed.

He was.

Baying and rushing, a pack of dogs skittered down the trail behind Jeep.

Dad didn't look back. He sent the Appaloosa surging forward, jumping ahead to level footing. Then, Dad turned Jeep to face the dogs.

And they were dogs, not coyotes or wolves. Black, white, speckled, and tan, the dogs moved in a blur. Sam couldn't tell how many there were. Four? Maybe five?

They circled silently now, except for loud sniffing. Could the hounds be planning their next move?

Sam pulled Ace to a stop. His forefeet danced. Did he want to bolt forward or retreat? Sam sat hard in the saddle, reins snug.

"Dad's got enough to worry about," she whispered to Ace.

Dad had Jeep under control, but the Appaloosa was scared. He tossed his head, straining the horsehair reins in a straight line to his hackamore. His pink-rimmed eyes rolled white and his hooves' staccato tapping said Jeep was barely setting each one down before jerking it up again.

Dogs were predators.

Horses were prey.

Jeep knew that speed was his only defense. He wanted to flee, but as long as the dogs weren't snarling or biting, he'd trust Dad's orders. He wasn't allowed to bolt.

Sam knew why. If Jeep ran, the dogs would be on him.

"Get outta here!" Dad shouted at the dogs. "Go on, get!"

One dog fell back, hearing the authority in Dad's voice, but another dashed ahead, brushing Jeep's forelegs.

Jeep started to rear as the largest of the hounds jumped up. Dad slammed his weight against the horse's neck, trying to keep him down, so he'd have the balance of all four feet.

With a low whinny, Jeep obeyed. Suddenly Dad gripped and lifted his coiled rope. In a backhand smack, he struck at the big dog, but not before it nipped the Appaloosa's nose.

It was too much.

Jeep was stronger than Dad was heavy. He soared into a full rear, nose dripping blood. When the speckled hound leaped a second time, as if going for the horse's throat, Jeep tried to stand even taller. Then, he fell.

Dad! Sam thought. Fear tightened her throat. She couldn't yell, but she gave a kick and Ace galloped straight toward Jeep.

Sam had never seen Dad be thrown from a horse.

Hands tangled in Ace's mane, she leaned low, holding tight in case the dogs turned on her.

She'd fallen before. She'd seen Jake thrown, too. But not Dad. Ever.

A yelp split the rustling sounds of paws and claws. The pack was running away.

By the time Sam pulled Ace to a stop, dust hung in the hounds' wake. They'd retreated up the hill, back the way they'd come.

"Don't get down!" Dad warned her.

His voice lashed so loudly, Ace shied and sniffed, sucking in a wind scented with dogs and Jeep's blood.

When Jeep lurched to his feet, Dad held his reins, keeping the horse between himself and the hillside.

The Appaloosa blew through his lips, calmer now that another horse was near.

"You did pretty good," Dad said, giving Jeep's

neck a hearty pat. Using his shirtsleeve, Dad swiped at Jeep's nose. "That cut's no big deal," he told the horse. "You'll forget about it before long."

Standing beside Jeep, Dad gripped both reins in his right hand while he slid his left over the horse's shoulder. He closed his eyes and grimaced, squatting instead of bending from the waist, to run his hand across Jeep's chest.

Dad's eyes darted from the hillside to Sam to his search for more wounds on the Appaloosa.

"Pretty excitin' there for a minute, wasn't it?" Dad asked Sam. His smile was white against his sun-browned skin, but Dad's eyes weren't happy. They weren't even relieved.

Sam's breath gusted out.

"Pretty terrifying," she corrected him. "Are you all right, Dad?"

"I'm kicking myself for being a fool. I never should have taken the scabbard off my saddle."

Sam shivered, and this time it wasn't from her damp clothes. When cougars had roamed the foothills last fall, Dad had put a rifle scabbard on his saddle. That was the only time she'd known him to ride out armed.

Did that mean he would have shot the dogs? Would he call Sheriff Ballard and have him capture them? Or would Dad think it was a one-time accident?

She didn't recognize the dogs, but maybe he

would. Before she could ask, Dad took in her soaked clothing.

"What happened to you?" Dad asked.

"Ace decided to go for a swim," Sam said absently.

Dad wasn't moving right. He gave a short, humorless laugh. He pressed his lips together in a hard line as he lifted his boot toward Jeep's stirrup.

"Did Jeep fall on you?" Sam asked.

"Didn't you hear the yelp? He fell on that black-and-tan hound. Don't know how bad he hurt him, but that's what sent 'em runnin'."

Vaguely, Sam remembered the cry of a frightened dog. Next, she realized Dad hadn't really answered her.

"Maybe you should stay here and let me go get Gram, so you could ride back in the car," she suggested.

"Maybe I should, but then Jeep would think something had gone wrong," Dad said. "It could turn him spooky around dogs, and then what? If there's one thing we don't need around here . . ." Dad's voice trailed off, then he looked up and gave Sam a wink. "If I ride him in as usual, he might forget all about it. When I doctor his nose, he'll wonder what the fuss is about."

"Okay," Sam said dubiously.

Dad's boot was in the stirrup and he was about to swing his leg over for the other stirrup when Jeep shied off a step.

"Knock that off," Dad ordered.

His sternness turned the Appaloosa statue still, but Sam saw a pale ring around Dad's mouth.

She'd been right. Dad was in pain.

"Dad, are you sure?" she asked as he gathered his reins.

"Let's go," he said, and Sam rode after him.

Read all the Phantom Stallion books!

AVON BOOKS

An Imprint of HarperCollinsPublishers

www.harperchildrens.com